EMMELIE PROPHÈTE

Cécé

Translated from the French by Aidan Rooney

archipelago books

Copyright © Emmelie Prophète, 2020
English language translation copyright © Aidan Rooney

First published in French as *Les villages de dieu* by Mémoire d'Encrier
First Archipelago Books edition, 2025

All rights reserved. No part of this book may be reproduced or transmitted
in any form without the prior written permission of the publisher.
Library of Congress Cataloging-in-Publication Data available upon request.

ISBN: 9781962770415

Archipelago Books
232 3rd Street #A111
Brooklyn, NY 11215
www.archipelagobooks.org

Distributed by Penguin Random House
www.penguinrandomhouse.com

Cover art: Pascale Monnin

The authorized representative in the EU for product safety and compliance
is eucomply OÜ, Pärnu mnt 139b-14, 11317 Tallinn, Estonia,
hello@eucompliancepartner.com, +33 757690241

This work is made possible by the New York State Council on the Arts with
the support of the Office of the Governor and the New York State Legislature.

This publication was made possible with support from the Hawthornden Foundation,
the Carl Lesnor Family Foundation, the National Endowment for the Arts, and the
New York City Department of Cultural Affairs.

PRINTED IN CANADA

Cécé

Outside, the usual racket. My body counted the imagined comings and goings. I had nothing but the present and stories with no beginnings. It was dark. I had slept lightly, just enough. No dreams, no real rest, just a short transition between two wounds.

For five days now the man had come. He would knock discreetly, always at the same time, 6:30 P.M. He was fat, acted shy, and wore striped shirts like the kind the tailor on Rue Ficelle used to make. His pants were hiked in the rear, the inseam too short or his belly too flabby for them to sit at his waist. His shoes were clean and well-polished with thick rubber soles. He wore the same clothes every time I saw him. His cologne was very strong, and clung to the pillow and the sheet.

I was never in the mood to talk to him. If our eyes met, he would smile. Not me. I never encouraged conversation. I'm sure he would have welcomed it.

He undressed timidly and slowly, embarrassed by his body. And he was ugly. He had short legs and his gut appeared even bigger when he took his shirt off. He floated a little in his white briefs that had seen their share of washings. He must have had a mother or wife obsessed with scrubbing clothes, especially whites, like my grandmother was. She was capable of soaking old undershirts and socks for several days in a basin of bleach-water and still not being satisfied with the result.

He was heavy on top of me. He hurt me. He didn't moan, didn't speak, and when he came, he tensed, making him even heavier. He would get dressed right away and hold out one thousand gourdes, double my price, wrapped in a piece of paper. I appreciated the thoughtfulness. I'd stopped counting the money. He basically had a tab. And I didn't think him capable of being dishonest. Call it intuition, that's all.

There weren't all that many clients. I spent my time on the rocking chair that had belonged to Grand Ma, fiddling with my phone, surfing Facebook. I was all over social media. Lots of people followed what I posted and took the time to comment, going to the trouble of disagreeing with me, even getting angry with me.

I wasn't afraid. I was used to the sound of gunfire. I grew up here in this Cité that's never seen a truce and where death can strike anytime, day or night. It's been nine months since Grand Ma died, from fear. It was a particularly rough night, a Sunday, that had started out calm until the rumor went around that a few guys in Makenson's gang had whistled at the girlfriend of a bigshot member of Freddy's gang as she was walking home from church. The two gangs that ran the Cité were never short of mutual provocations but there had never been, until that Sunday night, a direct confrontation. I'll always remember my grandmother's bulging eyes and her hands squeezing my wrist.

"Grand Ma, you're hurting me!" I had cried out.

"Cécé, Célia, my child, *piti mwen*," she wheezed. "Cécé, I feel like my heart's about to explode. I'm dying."

I slept in the same bed as Grand Ma. Always had. I knew right away when she died. She'd gone stiff. Cold. I couldn't, as I always had, put my right leg over her to help me fall asleep. I started talking to her

I don't remember what I said, except for some prayers she had taught me. I couldn't hear the sound of my voice. The gunfire was constant and the clamor went on till dawn.

I went to wake up Uncle Frédo. The noise I made opening the wooden door and nearly breaking the latch didn't disturb him. He was completely drunk, as usual. I couldn't rouse him so I went to knock at my neighbor Soline's door. She agreed to come back with me, almost shoving me to make me go faster. To her I was nothing but a little liar. How could I claim that Grand Ma was dead when only yesterday they had been at Mass together and she'd been just fine!

Soline had paused at the doorway, her large breasts floating in a floral nightgown. Like everyone in the Cité, she hadn't slept. She had dark rings under her eyes. Then she took a firm step over the four-inch threshold that Grand Ma had had built between the little porch and the front bedroom entrance so that rainwater wouldn't enter the house.

"She really is dead," I managed to stammer as we entered the room.

"Hush, *petite*," she replied, her eyes opening wide.

"Christa! Christa!" she cried, feeling Grand Ma's brow and neck before letting out a scream.

Tears ran down her round cheeks. I started to cry too, then launched into the keening you always hear when someone in the Cité dies. Neighbor Soline put her large, rough hand over my mouth and said, sobbing: "*Petite*, are you trying to wake up Freddy and his men? They only just went to bed. At your age you should understand these things."

I nodded as Soline, both hands on her head, skipped around the room, repeating *"Bon Dieu Ô! Bon Dieu Ô!"*

Uncle Frédo, almost as dead to the world as his mother, was snoring in the little bedroom whose door I'd forgotten to shut. It was empty except for a small iron bed and an old fuchsia-colored suitcase containing the few pieces of clothing he owned.

The Cité was quiet again. Freddy's gang had beaten Mackenson's. They were saying thirty deaths. Complete capitulation. Summary execution for the stubborn ones who refused to lay down their weapons. One gang only, one *base*, as they called it, would now be calling the shots in the Cité of Divine Power, and it would be Freddy's.

Neighbor Fany had called the funeral home. They arrived two hours later in a van that looked like the ones that ran between Boulevard Jean-Jacques Dessalines and Martissant, and on the front of which was written "Divine Grace." Neighbor Soline had put on an apple-green men's shirt over her floral nightgown, and a pair of long pants underneath. She looked odd under all these layers, and I couldn't help but think of all the crazy clownish characters who circulated during Kanaval – *la mayotte*, we called them – and who frightened me when I was little.

As usual, Neighbor Soline had all the say, and grief had given her even more authority. She told us to wait 'til 3 P.M. before starting to mourn. Joe, Edner, Fany, Fénelon, and his wife, Yvrose, agreed.

Rigor mortis had set in and made it impossible to close Grand Ma's eyes.

"In two or three days you'll be able to," said the funeral home worker as he transferred Grand Ma from the bed to the stretcher with the help of his assistant and the dexterity of someone who's spent a lot of time with corpses.

Uncle Frédo woke up. He looked old for a man of thirty-eight. He had slept in his clothes, now disheveled, and he smelled of booze. When they covered Grand Ma's head with the white sheet, he started screaming hoarsely, "Mama, Mama, Mama!" and Soline, Edner, Joe, Fany, Fénelon, and Yvrose told him in chorus: "Shut it! Shut up! Shut the hell up, you foolish *tafiateur*! You'll wake up the gangsters."

Uncle Frédo threw himself on the ground and started to moan softly.

Grand Ma had this house built herself. She loved to talk about it given half a chance. In the evening if she heard an odd sound on the roof, usually just rocks thrown by some bored kids, she would sit up in the bed and address the intrusion in a clarion voice.

"I built this house all by myself. I have no debt. I buy nothing on credit. I demand peace and quiet."

Her monologue could go on for several minutes, and she made sure all the neighbors heard her, Soline to her right, Fénelon and Yvrose to her left, Nestor out back, Pastor Victor and his wife Andrise a bit further on, Fany and her sister Élise in the house across the way, and whoever was passing by, whoever might have a reason to envy or resent her.

She used to tell me that when she had bought the plot of land forty years earlier, hardly anyone ever passed by. It was nothing but bushes, and her closest neighbors lived nearly five hundred meters away, a man named Joachim, his wife, and their daughter. All three of them were so old it was hard to believe she was their daughter. Grand Ma was never sure if the seller had really been the owner. No survey had ever been done. She'd built these two rooms with the help of Rosia's dad, Rosia being my mother, and moved in. More people came after that, at a frenetic pace, and put up makeshift shacks, leaving little alleys to get around. The government never protested, never bothered to get involved.

My mother was born in the big room, with the help of a midwife. My grandfather had already left.

"With some stuck-up tramp of a girl. Nothing to her name and already mother to four kids." There was no stopping Grand Ma once she got started. The passing years did nothing to diminish her anger.

Of my mother, only two likenesses remain. One is a small, yellowed ID photo taken when she was six years old for her school enrollment. She's staring into space, probably intimidated by the photographer. She looks sad. In the other, she's standing to the right of Grand Ma, who's seated in a large chair, with Uncle Frédo to her left. No one is smiling. They're all rigid. The background image is a waterfall. Water, grass, rocks ... a landscape that should be charming but isn't. My mother, Rosia, is wearing a long pink dress with straps and ruffles that go down to her white stockings. Her shoes are black. Grand Ma is dressed in a white outfit and heeled sandals. She has a small purse on her lap. The purse is still in the dresser. Uncle Frédo has on a white suit and a small red bow-tie around his neck, his shoes are well-polished, and he's standing up straight. He's four and Rosia eight.

I look a lot like my mother. When I was little, I'd stand up to Grand Ma and say that it was me. That made her laugh. A sad laugh.

My mother died when she was twenty. I was two and have no memory of her. Not even a smell. Nothing.

"I think she caught that dirty disease," Grand Ma would whisper, by which she meant AIDS.

Pastor Victor and his wife Andrise came to explain to her that evil forces had killed her daughter and were killing lots of young people like her in the city. But Grand Ma was no fool. The young doctor she had met at the General Hospital – very clean, honest-looking, and so nice she prayed to God right there that Frédo would become like him – had told her it was AIDS.

Rosia was already in pretty bad shape when she'd finally taken her to the hospital. She'd been wasting away for several weeks and my grandmother was worried. The young doctor asked only affirmative questions, already sure of his diagnosis.

"You've lost a lot of weight? You have trouble swallowing?"

"You have frequent diarrhea, and vomiting?"

"You have lesions on your skin? You've been coughing?"

He was handsome and impassive. He recommended tests, just to be sure, and that the girl, given her state, be hospitalized. Grand Ma had no money. The public hospital was on strike. The young doctor sent Grand Ma to one of his colleagues at the Health Center in Portail Léogâne who gave her some serums for free, medicine that would help Rosia feel better. She died a month later.

Grand Ma said she regretted not beating her, not keeping her away from the hoodlums who had convinced her to drop out of school at fifteen, after a chaotic trajectory. She could have been like that young doctor who had given them the medicine. She could have gone to college. But she started drinking and taking drugs, and got herself pregnant at eighteen with no idea who the father was.

"Anything can happen when you're high all the time," said Grand Ma.

Whenever Grand Ma chewed her out, and slapped her, Rosia would leave home for days.

"I did everything to protect you, though," Grand Ma would whisper as she stroked my hair. "I always kept you close, even if it suited your idiot of a mother. You'll sleep against my back until you're all grown up and settled. I won't let anyone take you away from me. I've already paid my price with your mother."

The days following Grand Ma's death were awful. The fighting started up again that very evening, this time between Freddy and dissidents in his own gang. The neighborhood was closed off, and hardly any cars went by on the main street. I slept under the bed. Uncle Frédo stayed sober for four days. His regular drink suppliers weren't doing their rounds.

Grand Ma's death went by unnoticed. So many young men were being shot every day, their friends rushing to bury them on the spot.

"They're soldiers. And soldiers should always be ready to die," said Pierrot, a young guy, maybe nineteen, who'd always stop in to buy Grand Ma's fried dishes.

After four days, the shooting stopped. Freddy himself had killed the traitors who'd rejected his authority.

"Bullet to the head, pow," said Pierrot excitedly, in admiration. "He's a real leader, hardcore," he kept saying.

He wanted everyone to hear the story, and no two versions were the same. It gradually got blown way up, filled with horrifying details. The gorier it got, the more Freddy's legend incited fear, the more respect he won. He knew that a rebellion on the other side of the ravine was already stirring. Pierrot was a spokesman of sorts for the gang leader, loyal and passionate.

I'd looked everywhere in the dresser, in the house, for things to sell to pay for Grand Ma's funeral. All I found was sixteen thousand gourdes, the entirety of her savings, squeezed into the old black purse that's on her lap in the family photo, completely cracked after all these years, and in the clear plastic pail that once contained paint and in which she used to stash the proceeds from her sales, three thousand piasters in dirty, tattered bills and coins. It was far from enough to pay for the funeral. I gathered the pots and pans to sell, the ones she'd used to cook the food she sold, and the sheets that were so well taken care of, bleach-white and smelling faintly of mothballs.

By the end of the day, I had sold only one pot for way less than what it was worth. The women at the market burst out laughing when they heard my prices, and let me know of better prices elsewhere, larger pots being sold on every sidewalk, in better condition, just arrived from Florida and even further away than that.

"Places you'll never visit, *petite*," they added.

Pierrot was a serious boy. Grand Ma used to compliment him on that. He always came back to pay for what he bought, "not like those hoodlums," she'd say, "who rob you of your bread and butter but you can't refuse to sell to them or they'll shut your operation down."

He hadn't heard about Grand Ma. He showed up the following Saturday, surprised not to find Christa on the little porch watching over her enormous and delicious-smelling pot of *griot* and rice with red beans, fried plantains, and what was undoubtedly the best *pikliz* in the city. He knocked loudly, and I came out to talk to him. He seemed sad. Genuinely.

"I'll talk to the Boss," he said in earnest. "He'll agree to help you."

Grand Ma's wake and funeral were quite grand. Freddy paid for everything. During the wake he even went so far as to accuse Makenson of having caused Grand Ma's death, and cast himself as her avenger. The whole time he kept his hand on a Glock 40, his good luck charm, and two of his associates stayed close to him, each carrying an AR15 semi-automatic assault rifle.

Freddy was tall and slim. He spoke slowly, and people only responded to him to agree. Neighbor Soline kept her head lowered and her arms crossed over her voluminous breasts. If she could have, she would have gotten up to show her contempt for the thug, that as a servant of God, she couldn't sit near an agent of the devil. But nobody dared contradict Freddy.

"I knew him when he was a baby," she'd explained to me that morning. "His mama is sister Julienne, a good Christian woman who lives in fear of God."

"It's his name that made him that way. His father had worked as a handyman for some Americans, one of whose sons was called Freddy, and so he wanted to give the same name to his own bastard son, thinking it would bring him good luck in life. Except that it doesn't work if you're Haitian. In Creole, *Freddy* means "cold." Plus, the kid always had a snotty nose and he was skinny as a nail, and when the other kids started chasing him calling him *Ti Freddy* it drove him psycho. You have to be a nutjob to kill people, to voluntarily put bullets in their heads and brag about it. I've heard he shoots anyone who dares laugh in his presence, 'cause he thinks they're making fun of his name. He's why poor Julienne sold her soul. He gave her so much stuff bought with stolen money that she stopped holding prayer meetings at her house. She got an electric mixer, furniture, even a generator. Tell me, since when have people living in the Cité owned that kind of stuff?"

Neighbor Soline started to cry. I couldn't tell if it was for Grand Ma or for what happened to Julienne and her son. She ended by saying that she was going to pray that Christa's soul rest in peace. Poor Christa.

Freddy had assigned two soldiers to take care of everything, Pierrot and Joël. Pierrot took the eighty thousand gourdes to the Funeral Service, "Divine Grace," and Joël took care of buying alcohol for the wake. Yvrose had offered to provide tea and coffee, out of her own pocket.

Livio was master of ceremonies. He was a real pro when it came to livening up wakes. He'd line up the jokes and people were always happy to play along, laughing even before they understood what he was talking about. Lots of folks came, mostly neighbors and Grand

Ma's customers. Frédo slept on his chair, a whole bottle of Barbancourt rum already drunk. I'd seen him hide two more in his room after Joël brought in the cases that afternoon.

A wind fanned the flames of the small homemade kerosene lamps used to light the gathering. Freddy had closed off the two ends of the alleyway so that no motorbikes would disturb the ceremony, not that he needed to. With Freddy in attendance, no stranger would dare wander through.

The funeral was the next morning at Saint Anne's, a Catholic church. Soline was scandalized, but she couldn't tell Pierrot that he'd been wrong to go with "Divine Grace" whose visitation would be held at 7 A.M. He was simply following Freddy's orders. They'd managed to close Grand Ma's eyes, but her face was still frozen in fright. She was dressed in an impeccable white suit, which I'd found on a hanger in her closet, her only outfit for grand occasions. It was hot despite the early hour. Uncle Frédo, Soline, Yvrose, Fénelon and I were in the first row, and people came to shake our hands, crossing themselves before Grand Ma's body. I cried all the tears I had in me, and I wished I could press myself close to her, and sleep with her the way I had my whole life. Yvrose tried to comfort me. Frédo wore a crumpled jacket that was too big for him. I don't know if it was Fénelon or Nestor who had lent it to him.

"Who's going to take care of me now, Mama?" he mumbled like an idiot.

At the church, which was just a big tent with a galvanized iron roof, eleven caskets were lined up for a collective funeral. The priest, who was in a terrible mood, kept messing up Grand Ma's first name, calling her "Chrisla." Whenever someone dropped to the ground crying, I couldn't tell which of the eleven departed it was for, except for one young woman who wore a white T-shirt on which a young man's face had been printed, and on the back, "A Dieu Michelet." It was the trend to split up the word "adieu" and the new spelling was everywhere, on jerseys, banners, and walls, to say goodbye to loved ones, friends, gangsters.

Grand Ma was buried in the Main Cemetery of Port-au-Prince. I limped terribly because one of my heels had broken and my feet hurt. I wasn't used to wearing high heels.

The days trickled past, slow and heavy. Nine months. That's a long time. I didn't know a house could be cloaked in so much silence. Despite the occasional gunfire that still ripped through the night or wounded the day. Despite the constant noise and chaos of the Cité, arguments between neighbors, prayer meetings held night and day as if such persistence was necessary for God to restore some semblance of order and bring justice, to break his silence and answer prayers, however trifling they were.

Uncle Frédo drank less after Grand Ma died. He spent a lot of time in his little room looking up at the ceiling, like he was in interminable mourning. He barely ate. When I knocked on his door, he never answered, and when I entered anyway he looked at me with a weak smile that made me feel better.

I had trouble imagining Uncle Frédo as anything other than an emaciated body wrecked by drink, though he'd been an athlete in his day. He did obstacle racing, and the 400 meters hurdles was his event. Grand Ma used to tell how one day a member of the Athletic Federation came to the house to talk to her about her son's athletic performance. She'd been so embarrassed. No one from outside the Cité ever came to her house. There was no room. She had to push aside all the pots and pans and the big pile of plantains on the little porch to make room for the man's feet when he sat in the rocking chair. Frédo was a minor, so Grand Ma had to agree to let him go to the Olympic Games, which that year were held in Atlanta, in the States. The man also explained to Grand Ma that it was the one-hundredth Olympics. She didn't understand what that meant, didn't know what the Olympic Games were, either. The only thing she retained was that her son Frédo could leave, and was going to take a plane, which made her very proud, especially after she'd given him a hard time for neglecting his lessons and running around like an idiot at the risk of getting run over by a car or injuring himself irreparably. "Glory be to God," she'd said, in the presence of the Haitian Olympic Committee representative, thanking him warmly, and trying her best to come across as a dignified woman and show that Frédo had a proper mother.

After the visit, Grand Ma took to telling everyone who came to buy food from her and everyone who went to church with her that her son was leaving for the United States to represent his nation in the Olympic Games, and she didn't know if he would be coming back.

"Maybe he'll decide to study in that wonderful country," she'd continue with a sigh, acutely aware of other people's jealousy.

Grand Ma was fond of remembering that first week in July, how she had run all over Port-au-Prince and spent her hard-earned savings on getting Frédo undershirts, socks, a pair of black shoes, and button-up shirts so he wouldn't have to go with the disgusting T-shirts he wore all day long.

    Claudy was Frédo's best friend. He lived in Carrefour-Feuilles. He did track and field, too, which is how they had bonded. They would go out for 5 A.M. runs, jumping over whatever obstacles they came across, from trash piles to old abandoned car engines, weaving around the wares of merchants who yelled at them and threw stones, calling them every name in the book. Claudy was very slim, even more so than Frédo, with the face of a boy who hadn't hit puberty yet. Grand Ma doubted that he was really seventeen. He looked closer to thirteen and played up his confidence to seem older. He was planning on staying in the United States with his godmother, who had no children, and who openly encouraged Frédo to stay too. Secretly, Grand Ma hoped he would. Why couldn't she have a loved one who lived in a foreign country? Something to give her hope, and let her imagine herself in one of those faraway, beautiful, and rich countries where, people said, it was easier to make money.

    Grand Ma confided in Old Nestor, whose daughter had been living in the States for fifteen years now, without ever coming home because she never got her papers. She hadn't been able to attend her mother's funeral, nor that of her younger brother who had joined the Cité Bethlehem gang, led by Big Elijah, and been killed in a shootout with the police.

"God is in control," Grand Ma had told Nestor to console him, thinking how she'd prefer her daughter to be far away in another country, illegal or not, than here, shooting up from morning to night with other degenerates.

And meanwhile Frédo started fantasizing about Atlanta, the United States, the lights, a place where he could both continue his studies and become a great athlete. Grand Ma heard him twisting and turning on the iron bed in the little adjoining room. She was used to this flawed form of communication. The creaking in his sleep revealed how tormented he was, somewhere between the joy of this new adventure, participating in the Olympic Games, and the decision he would have to make to stay, to escape, with Claudy, from the team. He was just a teenager after all, brought up like most boys who never had to figure things out for themselves. He sensed that Grand Ma was okay with it. But maybe she should have said something? She'd never talked to her children, not really. All she owed them was to meet the basic needs for which her meager income could allow. Yes, she'd dreamed of a better neighborhood for them, a nicer house, that they finish school, but she had always been a single mother. The two men with whom she had tried to make a life had left her, each leaving her one child to whom they hadn't even offered their last names.

There was no doubt in Grand Ma's mind. Leaving meant a better life for Frédo, for his mother, his older sister. Someone needed to try to save Rosia, to make her understand that she needed to be ready to change her life at any moment, that soon her brother would be able to send money to his family. At least once a month, Félicienne, the neighbor down the street, received a transfer from her son Baptiste who lived in New York. She'd even been to visit him, and said things about the city that were hard to believe. No blackouts ever, the fridge always stocked with food, suspended highways, buildings that almost touched the sky. Four years since she had visited and she still walked with her nose in the air. That flamboyance, that pride, Grand Ma thought, was also what people went looking for in those countries. Frédo might be her only chance of ever getting there.

She went through hell to get Frédo his passport, even with the help of the National Federation. She had to get his official birth certificate, which was ridiculous given that it was the government that issued it in the first place, wait in line at the immigration office, and wait four months for the passport to be processed. She clutched it so tightly, that navy blue booklet gold-embossed with the Haitian coat of arms. She brought it to church, begging God to shadow her son on whatever path he took, and above all to never let him forget his mother. And while he was at it, that God influence the arrogant consuls who might refuse her son a visa because he was a boy of the people.

The Federation took over at that point. Grand Ma wasn't allowed to accompany Frédo to the Embassy. Which she regretted. Not Frédo. Grand Ma sensed that he was embarrassed by her questions, her zeal, and the way she had of telling even people she didn't know that her son was going on a trip.

It was a Thursday. Frédo had told Grand Ma that he was leaving that Tuesday. He would not be wearing the shirts, pants, and socks she'd bought him but had to wear the delegation uniform. Grand Ma smiled and said he'd need them anyway, that he wasn't going to wear the red and blue jersey with the national flag embroidered on the left sleeve for the rest of his life. She should have taken him in her arms, but she'd never done it before, and plus her son was a man now and it was on him to protect her, to take care of her and his sister. He looked lost, with acne still on his face, his young body all muscle, and hair that she wished he'd kept shorter, but she'd decided to say nothing that might sound like disapproval or a reproach.

She went with him to the airport. They didn't speak much on the bus. It would have been hard with the blaring music. The loudspeakers echoed in her heart. She was the one dragging the suitcase. He'd made a sullen face when he saw the color she picked. Fuchsia. Grand Ma hadn't realized that this kind of detail mattered to a boy, especially one about to enter the world of sports.

She had never set foot in the airport. She didn't go inside. She wasn't allowed. Members of the delegation were waiting at the entrance, and recognized each other quickly thanks to the team gear. Claudy was already there. Frédo didn't get to hold his passport. The delegation head was to carry them at all times. He never even got to see the visa stamped in it. The team members chatted excitedly, ignoring the people around them, including Grand Ma, a couple who had accompanied their daughter, and a stylish, camera-toting young woman who took pictures of them from every angle.

Frédo had felt a little ashamed of Grand Ma. She'd put no effort into her appearance, and was wearing a dress that was too tight. She'd gained some weight but kept the same clothes, and her sandals showed her fat toes, the nails eroded by fungus. Before he disappeared into the terminal, Frédo gave her a quick kiss on the right cheek. She returned home and was frightened by the silence that set in, despite the agitation of the Cité and all the work she had to do before her customers showed up.

Haiti didn't get a single medal. Most of the athletes decided not to come back. Had they even concentrated on what they'd set out to do? Taking their passports proved no deterrent. It was hardly the first time. The Federation chose to remain silent on the matter. Grand Ma too. She heard nothing from Frédo and almost wished that Rosia would not return home either. During their last argument, she had tried to hit her daughter, but Rosia, under the influence of who knows how many substances, wasn't having it and hit back. Then it was Grand Ma who ended up crying in a corner when Rosia left, taking all the money she could find.

"Frédo is doing fine where he is," she'd say when anyone asked after her son. She really believed it, too. Why wouldn't he be, after all, even if he never sent word and seemed to have erased his past. He was better off. He wasn't in the same hole as Rosia, wasn't hanging around with gang members spreading terror, little thieves robbing the neighborhood merchants blind.

The days slid by. Grand Ma divided her time between church services and her business. She took on a young assistant, Mimose, who worked a full day on a small salary, purchasing produce, preparing food, and tending the fire. There's always someone poorer than the poorest. At least the job kept her fed, and sent her home with a share of whatever wasn't sold. She was twenty-three, already had three kids, and was packed in with them and her parents in a hovel two alleys over. She was a good worker, and Grand Ma, who felt very alone, appreciated her company.

Célia. Cécé. People often tell me that it's a pretty name. Three months ago I turned twenty. My mother, Rosia, hadn't picked out any names when she was pregnant. She was probably barely aware that she was bringing a child into the world and clearly being sincere when she told her mother she didn't know whose baby it was. She was just a teenager when she got into drugs and alcohol. Fourteen or fifteen. Grand Ma never saw it coming, too wrapped up in "finding life," as she put it.

Rosia came home in the sixth month of her pregnancy. She kept drinking, smoking, and taking drugs, whatever she could find. She stole from her mother to feed her addiction. Grand Ma told me that she prayed a lot that I would come into the world spared of a birth defect.

I was born so small they had to keep me at the hospital for two weeks. The doctor warned that I was at high risk for disease. He was wrong, but I stayed stunted. I'm five foot one and not very pretty. It must be because of the drugs.

And, yes, Célia was the name of the baby formula that Grand Ma bought at the Mercidieu grocery store, the biggest in the Cité. The sign reads "grocery," but it's really just a shop that sells everything from infant's milk to kerosene for lamps. When Grand Ma asked Rosia what she wanted to name me, Rosia looked at the small table that held three bibs, a bottle of water, and a can of Célia formula. She replied: Célia. Grand Ma had smiled. She thought it was a pretty name. "Célia Jérôme," she repeated three times, as she prepared my bottle. The doctor who'd deliver me at the hospital forbade my mother to breastfeed me. He'd caught her drinking a rum *tranpé* that she'd secretly bought near the School of Science not far from the hospital. Rosia couldn't have cared less. She wanted nothing to do with me. She couldn't wait to get back to her friends who spent their time in the streets begging for money to obtain what happiness meant to them. Freedom.

She was back to her old ways three weeks after I was born. Grand Ma was angry and asked her not to get herself pregnant again by a good-for-nothing just like her.

Rosia came by the house from time to time but never showed the slightest interest in me. Grand Ma was pleased that she kept her distance, what with the way she stunk, reeking of liquor, her hair a mess, and a cigarette forever in hand. She wanted money. Always. And Grand Ma paid to be rid of her. Grand Ma was my real Ma. She was happy to have me. With no one else in the house since Frédo had left, I brought her tremendous joy. She learned to talk with me, to express tenderness, something she had never been able to do with her own children. I advanced less quickly than other babies. I walked at sixteen months. Grand Ma was at her wits' end, and cursed her addict of a daughter.

Then Rosia came back to live with her mother as she waited to die. She brought her fatigue, her excesses, her misery, her sickness with her. Grand Ma put her in Uncle Frédo's room. There was no question of her sharing her mother's bed, since that was my place. She vomited up her life, spent of all energy. They didn't talk. This was a daughter who'd defied her mother and had even struck her once. Grand Ma was surprised that none of Rosia's binge-drinking friends came to see her. No doubt they were dying from the same disease, or else were too drunk and high to make it out the door. Or had they simply forgotten her?

Rosia died on Easter. I had just turned two. Grand Ma always talked about her grief during the years my mother was alive and in the grip of narcotics, but she never lingered on the heartbreak her death had caused. Maybe she'd long accepted it as inevitable.

"At least, she made you," she would say. "She chose to leave you to me. Thank you, God. Thank you, Heaven."

Cécé. Célia. I am a girl with a very ordinary story. My mother was my grandmother. She's the only family I ever had. At least until Uncle Frédo came back from his trip, though he'll always be more of a distant relative, like one of Ma's cousins who would visit from Maniche, not far from the city of Cayes, in the south. Those women would sometimes hold back, having lost the thread of their relationship with this cousin who had settled in the capital and built a house there. Tonton had so few moments of lucidity that, one day, Ma swore she must have done something wrong to be paying so dearly now through her children. At least he was there. He did his drinking at the house, slept off the alcohol there too, letting his mother take care of him, despite her age, making her responsible, guilty almost, for bringing him into the world.

I started school very late. Ma was afraid that the other children would break me in two, or maybe more, pieces. I think she wanted to keep me by her side as long as possible and would have liked to see me not go to school at all. I would hear her say to neighbors surprised that I hadn't started primary school yet: "Cécé is a sick child. Look how tiny she is. I've already lost Rosia. I don't want to run any risk with her."

In truth, she thought that school was a place of perversion, all the while hoping that I would become a doctor. It was at school that my mother had fallen in with a crowd who'd gotten her into alcohol and drugs. Maybe I had inherited some bad tendencies from my mother who, in turn, of course, had inherited them from her father. But I felt just fine. I understood everything. I knew all the bad words and could shock any adult, even Lorette, the crazy lady of the Cité who insulted everyone and would take all her clothes off whenever someone angered her or simply because she was having a bad day. Or Dodo, the raging alcoholic who sang his head off morning, noon, and night, and swore at anyone who told him his wife had left him because he couldn't get an erection. Ma had no idea that I was roaming the Cité alleys when she went to do the shopping, leaving me with Mimose, who, meanwhile, was getting groped by Fénelon in Ma's bedroom, maybe in her bed.

Ma resigned herself to bringing me to see Maître Jean-Claude, who ran the little primary school at the entrance to the Cité, one day when I was very angry at Mimose for refusing me a cola and had outed her in front of Ma:

"You dirty whore, taking it up your fat shit ass from Fénelon!"

Ma didn't lose a second sending me into the house and then accused Mimose of teaching me bad language and exposing me to sex shows in her absence.

"An angel," she said, beside herself with anger, on the brink of tears, "you've corrupted a tiny little girl. And she's right, by the way. You are a whore!"

My grandmother gave Mimose her marching orders, and told her to come back at the end of the month to pick up what she was owed. She came back into the house trembling, smelling of goat blood, Saturday's typical meat, and rummaged under the bed for the basin in which we kept the toiletries, then put toothpaste on my toothbrush, pulled me by one hand out of the corner in which I was hiding, acutely aware of the words I'd said, and dragged me through the backdoor to the rusted tin outhouse that was our bathroom, and brushed my teeth with a vengeance. The brushing was like an exorcism, intended to purify the mouth from which such abominations had emerged.

That day, Ma prepared the food, sold it, and washed everything afterwards, all by herself. It was very late when she finally closed the door to go to bed. On Monday morning (it was late November), she took me to the Angels of the Cité school, which was run by Maître Jean-Claude, an affable man, businesslike, in his fifties, who refused no students, even at the end of the school year. They talked in his office for twenty minutes while I waited outside, seated on a chair and trying to get my feet to touch the ground to take my mind off the ribbons she had used to tighten up my hair.

The office was part of a large room sectioned off with particle boards that were warped and spotted with large water or oil stains, and which let through a good chunk of whatever conversation was being had.

I hadn't succeeded in touching my feet to the ground. My grandmother came out of the office with a sad smile, and told me: "That's it, sweetheart. You start school tomorrow."

She might as well have said that Rosia had died all over again. Maître Jean-Claude, as everyone called him, looked ridiculous, showing his long teeth blackened by tobacco and bad hygiene as he asked me: "What's your name?"

I wanted to say something about his mother, the most popular insult in the Cité, but the look on Grand Ma's face dissuaded me. I stammered, "Cécé, Célia Jérôme." He added that it was time to learn to read, write, and speak French. He started to say lots of things in French, none of which Grand Ma nor I understood. What did we care? Thankfully.

I, Cécé, for the first time, had a book and a notebook. I went straight into the first grade. I was the eldest in the class, but I came across as younger. The others were more advanced than me. They could read the alphabet correctly. Not me. That whole first week, I was preoccupied with trying to touch the ground with my feet while sitting on the bench. It was the first time in my life that I had to stay in the same position for a long time. I was bored. I needed to find *something* to do.

I sat between two girls, Natacha and Joanne. They didn't seem to like me very much. On the third day, Joanne started poking me in the ribs with a pencil she had just sharpened. It hurt a lot. I didn't cry. I almost never cried. About an hour later, she tried to do it again, but I grabbed the pencil out of her hands and stuck it into her left thigh. She let out a blood-curdling scream. Even Maître Jean-Claude came out of his office to see what was going on. She was crying and wriggling in her little pale blue skirt covered in blood. Natacha was so frightened she couldn't get out a word either. The schoolteacher Madame Sophonie panicked because the principal was surely going to think that she couldn't control her class, and Maître Jean-Claude, somewhat alarmed, pressed me to tell him what had happened. I just shrugged. They concluded that Joanne had thrust the pencil into her own thigh, a version of the incident that worked for everyone.

The following day, Joanne showed up with her mother, a corpulent woman whose fake hair was sewn on every which way. Maître Jean-Claude had me brought in from the class. He gave an explanation in

French to Joanne's mother, who understood nothing and was sponging her forehead with a tissue that left little flecks of white paper on her face, which honestly was not a good look. It must have been the hair making her hot. Every so often she moved her hand as if to speak, when Maître Jean-Claude gave her a chance, but not a sound came out. She didn't dare speak Creole and couldn't express herself in French. The director of the Angels of the Cité forbade speaking Creole. The school's reputation depended on it. All the poor bastards living in the Cité and thereabouts dreamt of only one thing: that their children would speak the language that gets you to the top.

I understood from Maître Jean-Claude's gestures and the repetition of the word *petite* that he was explaining to Joanne's mom that I was too little to have committed the act her daughter had alleged. He compared my height and weight to those of Joanne who was a good head taller than I was, not to mention a little chubby. The woman left, annoyed. Joanne and I were ordered to make up and sent back to class with a resounding, "No more funny business!"

She walked behind me. Limping. She was afraid. As for Natacha, she had been smiling at me all morning. They both wanted to make peace.

I repeated my first year. Second year too. It was no big deal. Lots of boys did too. Sandino, Billy, Peterson, Robinson, Maradona. In fourth year, I caught up with Natacha who had been sick for two years. We became friends. Joanne had moved to another cité though, and no one knew what had become of her.

Grand Ma agreed that I should take private lessons from my teacher my third year, finally understanding that it was the only way to get through a class in just one year. The teachers were more indulgent toward students who boosted their monthly income. Maître Jean-Claude went to great lengths to explain how the system worked to Ma, who had a hard time understanding. It must have been the strange language he spoke. A nonexistent Creole full of *r*'s and *e*'s, and intonations that intimidated Ma. The free dinner she offered him every Saturday must have been part of the tuition. The whole time that I attended The Angels of the Cité, he ate on Saturdays without paying.

"Cécé knows how to read," Ma would tell her customers, tears in her eyes. It took me a long time to comprehend that she had good reason to be emotional. She bought a television. It was on the small side. I spent a lot of time in front of it, mainly watching music videos. Ma didn't involve me very much in her food business. I was meant to study, so I could become a doctor or an agronomist. She took on Lana to replace Mimose and insisted that I watch TV inside instead of talking to her, but I had learned not to say curse words in Ma's presence, even if I knew plenty and didn't hold back with my friends at school where my reputation as a tough girl was already made.

At thirteen, I went to a protest. Maradona said that we couldn't let the election results be stolen from us. I wasn't aware that anything had been stolen from me, nor had I followed the elections, but I had a good time along the boulevard around people I didn't know who were very happy or very serious, chanting "It's the people's victory. We want this president!" They smashed windshields and shopfronts, pillaged a few small businesses, targeted surely for being complicit in the theft of the people's victory. "This time, we have the right one," I heard a woman say. "This country has waited far too long. This president will finally free us from our misery."

I received my certificate when I was seventeen, and left The Angels of the Cité for the co-ed Collège Bernardin de Saint-Pierre, also in the Cité, where I was supposed to start high school. The superintendent, a thin man with his tie always askew and a strap in his hand, explained to us that Monsieur de Saint-Pierre had been an eminent French writer, and that he was sorry that we did not know that. That made us laugh. I was seventeen but some of my new classmates were twenty-one, and a few of the teachers – poor students who had just gotten their secondary school diploma, or maybe not even – were around the same age.

I didn't like to study. I watched, as much as our ration of electricity would permit, Latin-American TV shows. Which is what the girls at school talked about mostly. I had a Facebook account. Ma couldn't buy me a smartphone, which I resented, a little anyway. She just didn't understand that I needed it to communicate, to see the world. She had the same phone I had, a basic model good for only talking. I'd go to the Cyber Center near the National Theater, a building side by side with a spectacular open sewer in which thousands of polystyrene plates and plastic bottles rotted. The connection was bad and I didn't have any photos of myself to post so I wasted time "liking" my friends' posts and photos and added my nasty take to debates where everyone let loose and tried to one up each other with stories of misery or idiocy.

I repeated sixth grade. I barely passed fifth. And I stopped going altogether when Ma died. No one asked me why I no longer went. No one really gave a shit, in fact. Maybe they assumed it was because of money too. Which was true. I wouldn't have been able to keep paying the six hundred gourdes a month that school cost but it didn't matter, because I'd had enough.

Up until I was eight you could have told me that the world began and ended in the Cité of Divine Power, and I would have believed you. I didn't have a single memory that wasn't attached to the Cité, and I figured that the rest of the world was just as noisy, cramped, and stinky. Madame Sophonie had told us that she lived in the third district of Port-au-Prince, the capital. The sea wasn't very far but I had never gone swimming, probably because it wasn't necessary. If it had been, Ma would have been devoted to it, same way she was to school, same way she was to church where she'd bring me once, sometimes twice a week.

An archway marked the entrance to the Cité, made by locals who call themselves "militants." Maybe one day I'll know the cause they're sacrificing themselves for. There was no official figure for the number of inhabitants, but there were lots of us and, every so often, we had to push back the Cité limits. Some homes weren't hard to build. Corrugated iron, wood, and a few tarps did the trick. Others, however, were impressive, constructed with hard materials over several stories. They included hot-sheet hotels, pawnshops, shops on whose fronts BAZAAR was written, morgues, schools, churches. There were confessionals all over the Cité of Divine Power, and at all hours of the day and night people prayed, taking turns in improvised temples endowed with incredible sound systems to chant and sing, as if it all should never end. The church closest to our house was run by pastor Victor, and that's where Ma went.

The Cité of Divine Power was essentially noise. Noises muffling other noises. Shots fired in broad daylight to frighten a shopkeeper who didn't want to pay the fee to the gang of the moment that was extorting him, radios on full volume, each broadcasting a different program, neighbors arguing, screams of children getting beaten, skinny little kids running around, playing, handicapped because of some accident or another or because their parents had drunk too much alcohol or smoked illicit substances during pregnancy, and who endured the cruelty of their friends, far too many kids, which testified to the elevated birth rate, the products of short-lived love affairs, rapes, or a miracle of God himself even. Young women who prayed all day long maintained in all seriousness that the Holy Spirit had impregnated them, and recounted their dreams to wide-eyed lost souls so desperate they would believe anything. The unhinged (all too plentiful), the drunks, the junkies, people crippled by the last earthquake or the victims of gangs, the blind, the departed, the grieving, the preachers who shook God's hand several times a day, vendors loudly selling their wares, the bony dogs who all looked the same sniffing everywhere in search of food, hopping along on three paws, one eye missing or with an infected wound because everyone let the stray dogs have it, for pleasure, out of habit, for something to do; throwing stones at them was a reflex shared by children and adults alike.

There was always a death to mourn in the Cité. Gang members would kill each other, or one would kill his own leader to take his place, plus there were frequent shoot-outs with the police that always left dead bodies. Of course, people also died from various poverty-related illnesses and "la belle mort" didn't exist, no matter what your age or disease. Death was always blamed on bad spirits and werewolves.

"Back then, I pretty much knew everybody, I'm telling you," Grand Ma used to say, looking around her, shaking her head nostalgically. The Cité had changed too much. As for me, I knew lots of people. Everyone who went to school with me, their friends, the friends of their friends, their parents, their dead, and people on Facebook. We talked a lot about the dead and a lot of people knew who would be next, because they'd joined such-and-such a gang, too poor, too fragile, or more mundanely because he had insulted a henchman in a rival cité who would seek revenge eventually.

I wasn't entirely wrong, though, in thinking that the world could be reduced to the Cité of Divine Power. The laws of the Republic stopped at the archway, a little before even, rendered impotent by the sheer dilapidation of a cité in which many inhabitants seemed to have landed without a past. To live here you had to believe firmly in the present and invent it every second.

Beyond the archway, there was the rest of the city, a place full of temptations that I promised myself to explore from start to finish. Once I went with my sixth-grade class on an outing to the mountains. There are places not too far away where the temperatures are cool, with beautiful houses and green spaces. There are almost no trees in the Cité. Neighbor Fany recycles paint cans that she keeps on her stoop and uses to grow flowers, basil and lemongrass, brewing teas to temper her grief. She never got over losing her fiancé, Pipo, who was a member of Fanfan le Sauvage's gang and got killed in a confrontation with Franzy Petit Poignet's gang, so called because his left arm was shorter than his right, a deformity that had earned him widespread mockery since childhood, leaving him bitter and cruel. Fany lived with her sister Élise, an old maid who was neither pious nor virtuous.

I knew the area around the Champ de Mars pretty well. I often snuck away from Grand Ma, whose greatest fear these past twenty years was that I'd stray like my mom, to go roaming with classmates who wanted to skip a French or math class. The walk was fairly long, and it was always hot, but the freedom reinvigorated us. We were on our way to a somewhere else that was very close and yet struck us as very far. We'd even go into the supermarket next to the Rex Cinema that had been gutted by the 2010 earthquake and into which people tossed their trash. We went wild at the sweets, the cold drinks, the fruit, but couldn't buy anything. The kids who came from the Cité had to have appeared strange. It must have been our shoes dirtier than other people's, our clothes, our manners, because every time we entered the supermarket a wide-shouldered man in khaki followed us with a grim look on his face. I went to Kanaval too. Once. With the help of Natacha who assured my grandmother that we absolutely had to do an assignment using dictionaries and maps she had at her place. Grand Ma looked at us anxiously until Natacha reminded her that she and her mom went to the same church. That Kanaval was beautiful. I drank my first beer. For days after I tasted its bitterness in my mouth. I was sixteen.

The Cité of Divine Power stank. It was probably all the mini-canals, standing water, and other things. Lots of other things. Our house always smelled like cooking fat, like food. Natacha's smelled of sulphate; her mother sold shampoo, soap, and products to whiten your skin, which Natacha had been doing since the sixth grade. Church smelled of sweat. Sweaty women and men who spent too much time there, who carried too much, literally and figuratively, who came to share those burdens with the Lord who was in no hurry to make them go away. Bernardin de Saint-Pierre High School smelled like a mix of things, like rotten household waste, because people were always tossing their trash over its walls. The school had tried all sorts of campaigns, threatening those who did the dumping, but it never worked. Soline's home smelled of the spices she sold: garlic, cloves, ginger. Fany's smelled of the booze Élise was always drunk on. In Fénelon and Yvrose's house, there was a meld of aromas from the array of products they sold in their shop, where I bought my notebooks on credit. Joe and Edner were masons whose wives didn't work. Their homes smelled of vomit and children's feces and sweat. Nestor's place smelled of old age, staleness, strips of wood that fell like ringlets from the planks he sawed and sanded to make little boxes to sell. And these odors came together and choked everyone in the Cité of Divine Power.

Uncle Frédo sent no word for twelve years. To me he was just the little boy standing to Grand Ma's left in the family photo. Whenever Grand Ma mentioned him she would stare into space, as if she were trying to imagine him in that huge faraway country of justice and infinite possibilities. She faulted him for only one thing: not sending any news to his mother. He didn't even know he had a niece. "We all need a family," she would say, her voice quivering.

Not one day went by when she didn't think of him. She didn't need to say anything. I could tell. She would turn her back to me so I wouldn't notice her reddened eyes, or her trembling bottom lip.

Had he been sick? Had he continued playing sports? Had he gotten a job? Had he married? Was he dead? Death was the only thing that could blanket a human being in such silence. Sure, she didn't have an address, like almost everyone in the Cité of Divine Power, but lots of people here had relatives abroad, and they always found someone returning home to whom they could entrust a letter, sometimes more, explaining which alleys to follow to the chosen messenger, who would figure it out just fine, asking around for the person being sought, giving their name and description. Take Old Nestor's daughter, who had had no trouble at all. And now that there were cell phones, all she had to do was give her number to the messenger.

"But you won't ever abandon your Grand Ma, isn't that right?"

"I will never abandon my Grand Ma," I'd always answer in earnest.

She would smile, and seem consoled. Grand Ma wasn't one to feel sorry for herself. We were better off than lots of our neighbors, we could feed ourselves, we had a house with walls and a galvanized roof in a sea of huts covered with tarps in which several people slept. She didn't pay the gangs much for the right to sell her wares, a few meals here and there, to some of the soldiers, and it was forgotten. She was just a single woman, and not a young one. An old lady of the Cité who they looked kindly upon.

Uncle Frédo reappeared one day in front of the house while Grand Ma was cutting plantains and sweet potatoes for the evening fry. She noticed that someone was blocking the light, but she didn't want to look up. If she let herself be interrupted by some lunatic or neighbor stopping by to talk about Élise's latest fantasy or how the cost of living had gone up again, she took the risk of not being ready when the first customers showed up. The shadow stayed for several minutes and said nothing. She finally caved in and looked up. The shadow was a very thin man in crumpled clothes, with a large afro, a full beard that was too long, worn out shoes, and a battered fuchsia suitcase, who was looking at her tenderly. Grand Ma let out cries that sounded like yelps. I dropped my Experimental Science textbook and raced outside, which is when I saw a man whom I took for one of the Cité's degenerates.

My grandmother stopped screaming and whispered, "Frédo, Frédo," as the neighbors came running to see what was going on. The slightest noise in the Cité of Divine Power could gather a crowd, except when there was gunfire. Frédo stepped forward, set down his suitcase, and laid a hand on Ma's shoulder as she wept. Everyone seemed stunned. This wasn't how a person returned from abroad after all these years. Christa must have been having us on this whole time, because this bum had clearly come straight from prison or the insane asylum.

Soline immediately ran home to prepare a teaspoon of olive oil and salt, which is the best remedy for a big shock, and had Grand Ma swallow it, all the while keeping a suspicious eye on the man who smelled truly awful.

"It's my little boy. It's my little boy," said Ma, sensing the discomfort caused by Frédo's presence.

The neighbors scattered, reproachful looks on their faces, leaving us alone.

"This is Rosia's daughter," said Ma, rubbing my back, without looking at Frédo. "Rosia died. Died, do you hear?"

She'd raised her voice and started to cry again, this time for Rosia's death. She needed to cry for her daughter in the presence of her son. It was the first time in my life that I witnessed her sorrow over my mother's death. Frédo smiled at me, a sad, wilted, gentle smile. He had wrinkles around his eyes and appeared old and tired. Grand Ma got up, prepared him a plate of rice, and softly told him that the meat wasn't ready yet. By the way he devoured the food, he must have been very hungry. Afterwards, he went into the little bedroom as if he had just left it yesterday, placed his old suitcase on the ground, and slept for two days and two nights.

Grand Ma was happy that her son was back. He had been deported from the United States. He explained this in a whisper as he ate, talking more to himself than to his mother. It was as though he was suddenly realizing what had happened to him. Grand Ma had seen plenty of young men return to the Cité labeled "deported" and therefore dangerous. Some joined gangs or adapted to their new life by taking something up, and they all had the same look on their faces. Sadness, hope, the need to go back to the country that refused them a second chance.

Frédo wasn't a criminal, or even a thug. He was a failed runner who couldn't clear the obstacles erected in front of him in a country where he couldn't gain a foothold. He'd failed from the outset. If only he had won a medal during the games! But he'd been terrible, Claudy too, nowhere near the level of the other athletes, and too obsessed with the life waiting for them outside the Olympic Village. All that light, that well-being within reach.

All that Frédo wanted once he came back was to pick up his life where he'd left off in 1996 and, why not, forget those terrible years when he'd wanted to die but lacked the courage to make it happen. And to carry out this voyage through time, or to forget rather, he drank and he slept. He refused to talk about his time spent in the United States. His mother understood it was better not to insist. Until the day she died, Grand Ma slipped him a few gourdes every morning, and then he got drunk. He ate only once a day, slowly, as if it pained him. His lower lip was completely pink, burned by the pure alcohol that went into the concoctions he picked up from multiple *tranpé* merchants in the Cité.

Then I was the one to give Uncle Frédo money. He never asked, but how would he manage otherwise? Besides, it was the least I owed to Grand Ma. Poor Uncle Frédo. It also spared me from having to explain the men I brought back to the house. Not that he ever asked. I'm sure he understood. What could he have said? Uncle Frédo was a nobody, a wreck, a lost soul, a thin body in soiled, ragged clothes.

There was shooting everywhere. Joël had killed Freddy. Unloaded his ARI5 into him. Freddy was dead but the others kept shooting him, letting out their rage, their jealousy, all the frustrations accumulated those many months during which they'd endured his sociopathic whims. He was a human rag by the time they threw him into a hole in the ground, near the candelabra-shaped cactus, along the path that led to one of the rare open spaces in the Cité which everyone called "the basketball court." An old hoop had been hung up, and kids practiced there every afternoon when it wasn't being used by the guys from Freddy's gang. They liked to play basketball, too, setting down their Galils to play a game, to enjoy whatever adolescence still remained in them, forget the corpses, the gunfire, the alcohol, the drugs.

Joël hadn't liked that Freddy had beaten up Pierrot and broken his arm. The gang leader had caught the kid sleeping when he was supposed to be keeping watch, and grabbed his weapon, kicking him and screaming insults about his mother. Joël tried to intervene. The kid was bleeding everywhere and begging forgiveness. Freddy smacked Joël in front of everyone, and called him pathetic and an idiot. Joël was angry. He felt like killing him. He needed to kill him. He dreamt about it for a full week. And in the end he took him by surprise. In cold blood. He told everyone how he saw Freddy writhing in his own blood like an animal, and finally glimpsed fear in the eyes of the man who for almost twelve months had been terrorizing the Cité, and beyond even, extorting government ministers, demanding payment not to block the roads leading south, to keep political rivals quiet.

The other members of the gang shot up Freddy's corpse to show immediate allegiance to his killer, to show Joël they were on his side and proclaim him their new leader right away. Whoever murdered the leader replaced him, inherited his stuff, his insanity, sometimes his mistresses.

I barely recognized Joël when I ran into him after he'd proclaimed himself king. I'd gone out to buy bread and corn grits at the corner market when our eyes met. He looked away. He was surrounded by ten armed young men. I knew all of them. They'd grown up in the Cité, and used to buy food from Ma. Pierrot had a pistol in his left hand, his right arm in a sling, his head wrapped in a red durag with familiar designs, the kind you find everywhere, especially during Kanaval. He pretended not to see me.

The young man who had brought the bottles of alcohol for Ma's wake had completely transformed. He was a man now, filled with rage, aware of his power and his own looming death, who could go anywhere in the Cité. The kind of man from whom people ask favors, begging him to spare this or that offender's life, or to threaten a school official into taking back an expelled kid. It could be very serious or very mundane, but the ability to solve a problem established the kind of leader you were dealing with, and built his legend.

Sister Julienne had quietly been told not to cry, not to reclaim her son's body, not to talk about him even. Soline went to see her. She found her looking dignified, surrounded by her nice furniture, her state-of-the-art household appliances, sitting in a very nice armchair, staring into space, mumbling that she accepted God's will and Joël's.

"A week since I've seen him," she said, "but God sees everything and knows everything."

"I have nothing but prayers to give you, my sister," said Soline.

She didn't respond, and Soline left. She was the only one who dared to visit her. The others, who used to swing by on occasion to leave a message for the Boss, to compliment her on her son's success and his intelligence, had disappeared or were too afraid of the new leader. Freddy was a past to be quickly forgotten. Only the present counted. And it went by Joël.

His name was Carlos. I might never have known. It would have changed nothing in my life. He was just a customer. I wished more were like him. Silent, happy just paying, not even asking for a glass of water, keeping their lives to themselves.

6:30 P.M. That punctuality could appear suspect in a country where people are never on time, and proud of it. It bothered me, in any case. I caught myself waiting for him. Last night he told me his name. Carlos. I felt like saying something hurtful, like why didn't he wear pants that fit, or button-ups without stripes. He'd never done anything to me. He'd offered to bring me something to eat every night from then on. I said no. I didn't want him thinking he had some obligation or special privileges. No one even needed to know that I "entertained." Well, that's what I wanted, but everyone knew everything in the Cité. Nothing got by Élise. Soline would come see me sometimes. I didn't like the way she looked around, sniffing like she was trying to find something, and I was planning on telling her so. I was an adult now and intended to manage on my own.

I knew the type. People pretend to be helping, then become invasive and intrusive, guided only by self-interest. Like Fénelon.

The first time was with him. The old bastard who wanted to pray with everybody, always flanked by his skinny wife Yvrose, with her large head that she shared with the many children in the Cité born with hydrocephalus, her too-big flowery dresses, and her Bible stuffed under her arm.

Two weeks after Ma died, he came to pray with me to help me through my grief. Truly, his compassion knew no bounds! He started by touching me, couldn't have cared less that Tonton was snoring in the next room. He had an old man smell and his breath reeked of peppermint. I wanted to scratch him, bite him, spit on him. I thought about Mimose. I had seen him put his hand under her skirt, I'd heard her moaning like some filthy animal, and I'd watched as he slipped money into her hands. Poor Mimose. Deep down I'd always hated that hypocrite Fénelon.

I needed money, too. Like Mimose must have. I hadn't understood. I'd been too young.

"Not here," I said to him. "Let's go somewhere else. I feel like Grand Ma can hear and see me here."

He hesitated and smiled, exposing front teeth trimmed in gold and giving off a strong odor of mint. To mask the rot, I thought.

We set a time and a place. I was supposed to meet him the next day at the Lambi Hotel in Mariani. It wasn't that far away, but there were lots of traffic jams because of the stalls crowding the streets and public transportation vehicles stopping wherever they liked, and the piles of dirt and trash, especially bad during the rainy season. He'd given me a little money for transportation, just enough for the round trip.

"You'll get a lot more after," he'd said with a predatory smile and a waft of mint that turned my stomach.

I set out boldly. It was my first time leaving the Cité since Grand Ma's funeral. I put on my white sneakers, my blue jeans and a pink T-shirt. With my hair pulled back in a scrunchie, I looked thirteen or fourteen, and people called me *petite* or *ti chérie*, which is how you showed you were looking out for someone.

Fénelon arrived before me. The hotel was deserted. A spot slowly being forgotten, and covered in dust. A former establishment at the southern exit from the city that everyone seemed to have collectively agreed to abandon. I thought it was disgusting. It had conchs, which people call "lambi," stuck all over the walls, hence perhaps the hotel's name, Le Lambi. The receptionist, a gray-haired man, looked at me disapprovingly over his glasses. Now that the old establishment had become a love hotel, he'd probably seen lots of girls like me. I met his eyes bravely. I wanted to tell him I was older than I looked, but that what I was doing was none of his business, that I'd never had a dad.

Fénelon had left instructions. A young girl with a very slim waist who seemed completely indifferent to the world around her brought me to the room. Everything was brown and unlit. Turtle shells had been hung on the walls. Fénelon opened when she tapped on the door. The young woman left without a word. Fénelon smiled at me. I lowered my head. He was wearing a sleeveless white shirt and the soft wrinkled flesh of his arms wiggled. His brown pants were a little too big and held up by a belt with cracking fake leather. He had to have been older than Grand Ma.

The room resembled Fénelon. It hadn't changed, like the rest of the hotel. Granted, the houses in the Cité weren't much to look at, but here it felt as if time had stopped, that no one lived here. The room was wall-papered in yellow and brown, almost the same color as the floor tiles. The custom-built furnishings were wobbly.

I looked at myself in the mirror. It was old too, a little rusty from being near salt water, no doubt. My face was boney and, my god, how ordinary! I turned away to look at the picture hanging on the wall. A woman dressed as a peasant playing a drum. The sides of the canvas had pulled away. It was pretty ugly, really. Uninterested in the room's decor, Fénelon undid his shoe laces. A light knock sounded on the door. He got up to open it. It was the girl with the slim waist. She was carrying two Coca-Colas and plastic glasses with ice cubes on a tray, along with a roll of toilet paper. I'd have preferred a beer but Fénelon was too religious to drink alcohol or be with someone who did.

He moved towards me, still wearing his socks, the kind athletes wear, that must have been white in an earlier life and now were piss-yellow.

"My prinnn-cess," he murmured, as if there were three *n*'s in the word princess.

I got up abruptly and said I wanted to go to the bathroom. To get away from him. But I was perfectly aware that there was no escape. I went into the bathroom. It smelled awful. The toilet tank had no cover. It didn't work. There was a bucket filled with water intended to flush it.

When I came back out, he had a glass of Coca-Cola in his hand, had taken off his pants and was now displaying his dark blue underwear. It was too much for me. I closed my eyes and sat on the edge of the bed, which squeaked terribly. He pressed himself against me, repeating his "prinnn-cess." He turned me over on the bed that creaked so loudly I felt like it was crying on my behalf. He took off my shoes, my pants, my pink top, and my underwear with flowers on it. He grunted like a pig. He undressed, and I smelled his lukewarm, wrinkled body against mine which felt nothing.

He rubbed himself horrendously against me, torturing the bed, without managing to get an erection. Finally, he put two fingers into my vagina, and pushed them in as far as he could. I screamed from the pain. I hated that old pervert with every inch of my body.

I was sore. I'd bled a little. I got dressed without looking at him. I'd have to wash myself with a large bar of soap to get the smell of mint and drool off me, and I thought of Ma and how she used to brush my teeth furiously when I said a bad word. I now understood the ritual's purifying effect. I had to get back home right away.

Finally, I let myself look in his direction. He was sitting on the bed, his head in his hands. I saw his ribs, his wrinkled thighs. He was skinny.

"I used to be very good at this, you know."

I started when I heard his quivery voice. What did I care! I just wanted him to give me the money as promised so I could get the hell out of there. I opened the dirty yellow curtain with little pink flowers, and looked out the window at a narrow balcony, covered with conch shells, and at the sea beyond. They must have decimated the mollusks to get so many shells for the hotel. The sea was dirty. You could see islands of plastic bottles and other trash, and my vagina still hurt terribly.

I felt Fénelon's hands on my shoulder and pushed him away violently. There were traces of tears on his sunken cheeks. He was crying over his lost virility. He was completely distraught. I took all his money, leaving him the exact amount he'd given me for the round trip to Le Lambi: fifty gourdes.

I bought myself a phone and an internet subscription. The phone was a ZTE. It was the best value in smartphones, a dreamed-of object whose importance Grand Ma had never realized. Like Natacha, like Pierrot, like so many others, now I could take photos, open Twitter and Instagram accounts. I put all of Fénelon's money into that luminous object, a true window into things that had until then been inaccessible.

I thought a lot about Mimose. I wanted to try to find her. I'd felt dirty since the sordid business with Fénelon. I thought about setting fire to his home, to make him disappear, and forcefully erase the memory we shared. But I didn't dare. Yvrose had never done me wrong. Stalking him, and then stabbing him to death with the knife Ma used to cut her big chunks of meat also struck me as a good idea. But the plan quickly fell through; I'd never killed anyone. I thought about asking Pierrot but I would have had to explain everything. I understood that even dressing it with lies wouldn't remove the shame. For a whole week, everything smelled of mint. I felt nauseous.

I asked Livio if he remembered Mimose, if he knew where she was living. He was surprised that I remembered her. He smiled, showing teeth pocked with small black holes.

"She lives in Blessed Spring," he said, "where she runs her frying stall. She went to live there with her children after she left your Grand Ma. She met a man who lived there and took up with him."

It bothered me that Livio said she'd left Grand Ma. I wanted to explain what had happened, but didn't have the words, and Livio wouldn't have understood in any case. You didn't pour your heart out around here, unless you'd lost someone close. Before and during funerals, sobbing and moaning was acceptable, but afterwards you went back to your own pain, which was often more violent than death itself, the ultimate deliverance, that in some cases was wished for.

You had to take Harry Truman Boulevard to get to Blessed Spring, almost as far as Saint Bernadette's Church. Then, when you got off the mototaxi, you had to go down a breakneck slope. Blessed Spring was a massive slum, its few trees covered in dust, with plastic bags hanging from their branches like fruit. Each village had its own feeling. Blessed Spring wasn't as noisy as the Cité of Divine Power. You could hear a few prayer meetings, half-starved vendors sitting around almost everywhere and chastising kids who, with impressive dexterity, were rolling along an iron hoop and threatening to knock over the jars of milk, the old shoes racked on a trestle, and the kettle set on a small homemade charcoal stove in which was cooking, in boiling oil, the portion of the batter filled with herring, tomatoes, peppers, sometimes hard boiled eggs, *pate kòde*, which was being sold by none other than Mimose.

It hadn't been hard to find her. Her stand was near the entrance. She looked thin, with a yellow scarf covering her hair, and a black dress with traces of flour on it. I could tell from her knit brow that she was focused. The glowing fire gave off an intense heat, and ashes kicked up by the wind flew in her eyes and settled on the clothes of the people nearby. Two men, probably masons, and a young woman in shorts were waiting for their *pate kòde*.

She hadn't changed much. What was her life like now, apart from what you could see, what she let people see? I would have liked to talk to her, to tell her how much I regretted what I had done to her. She probably would have only vaguely remembered me, if at all. More than a decade had gone by since Grand Ma had kicked her out. I stood beside some customers and no one paid me any attention. It smelled really good, there were two *pate kòde* in a pot that was slightly too small, visibly turning from the pale yellow of flour mixed with saltwater to a golden color that made your mouth water. I ordered one. Mimose replied, without even lifting her head, that there weren't any more. She was out of flour. She didn't recognize my voice. Didn't recognize me at all. Maybe she had completely forgotten that episode in her life.

It was almost noon. I walked without really knowing if I was going the right way to get out of Blessed Spring. It didn't matter. I was going to hop on the first mototaxi that went by. It had calmed me to see Mimose.

I was famished when I met Carlos. I was coming back from pastor Victor's, where I'd gone to charge my phone. I always had my charger on me, because the battery drained quickly from all the time I spent on social media, but electricity was hard to find, the network constantly down due to illegal poaching, standard practice in the Cité, including our place. We'd always had electricity in the house, as far back as I can remember, and never once paid for it. Andrise, the pastor's wife, congratulated me on my new phone, and I didn't dare tell her how hungry I was. I told her I was good, that Grand Ma had left enough gourdes for now. She said that she prayed for me every day.

The sun was going down and my stomach was growling. I liked Rue des Ficelles, which was a paved street, one of the few in the Cité. I was leaning against a wall on which was painted an advertisement for an energy drink that claimed to boost men's sexual endurance when I heard someone stifle a laugh.

And there he was. Body squeezed into a striped shirt and gray pants.

"A young lady should not be leaning against an ad for a product like that."

"Or what?"

He laughed again, and started explaining that it was a thing against women.

"You ever try it?"

"Never."

"I can get you a can. The vendor on the corner sells it."

"I'd rather eat."

It came out just like that. He told me to follow him. We walked to the parallel street, and entered a little gazebo where some plastic chairs and tables had been set up. He seemed to have been there before. The owner came over and they exchanged a vigorous handshake. "Chez Morel" was painted on the backs of the white plastic chairs. Wednesday was soup day, the best soup in the Cité, according to Morel. Not that I cared, I'd have eaten anything.

It *was* good, though. The chilis in it made my nose run. It was an orgy of meats and whatnots that I couldn't identify, except for the plantains, which always gave me the hiccups because I didn't take the time to chew them. I couldn't finish my bowl, and asked if I could take the leftovers with me. I had to bring something back for Frédo to eat. I was all he had.

Carlos walked me home without my asking him to. We hardly spoke. We weren't going to continue our inane conversation about the drink that helped men have lasting erections. The only man I'd been with was Fénelon, and every time I thought about it I wanted to throw up.

I don't know what he was hoping for that first night, but I gave him a curt bye-bye in front of the porch. He came back the next day, around 6:30. I was sitting out front on Grand Ma's rocking chair, and had taken at least fifteen selfies without getting a satisfactory shot. He stood there watching me without saying anything. I asked him straight off if he had money. He paused before saying he did. I invited him in. It felt like he was obeying me.

He was gentle. He tried to kiss me, but I turned my head away. It was already dark, and I hadn't lit the kerosene lamp. The darkness suited both of us. He was heavy. He spent a long time touching me. Still no talking. I was grateful for that. I didn't like talking much. I had nothing to say. He asked me afterwards if I wanted to eat at Morel's. I said no. I'd rather he give me five hundred gourdes. He handed me a thousand. It was more than the minimum wage. It was more than most people in the Cité earned in a week.

There was no shortage of cités. Slums. Cesspools with rudimentary homes prone to absurd, nasty confrontations whose reasons remained largely unknown or were so unimportant that they were quickly forgotten.

Bethlehem was the closest cité to Divine Power. And enemy territory – at one time worth a short-lived alliance between Makenson and Freddy. But now the neighborhoods kept their distance, and everyone carried a weapon, "sleeves" as they called them. Gang members killed each other, often on outrageous pretexts. One of the bloodiest face-offs happened because Fanfan le Sauvage had started a rumor that all the members of Makenson's gang were queer. For them it was the worst insult possible. Even queers were against queerness – they were in fact the most vehement, radical, in their opposition. The inhabitants of the two cités had gone almost two weeks stuck inside their homes. Grand Ma had had to throw the pork she had bought for her business to the dogs. God only knows how long she tried to hold onto it, insisting that if she added enough spice, customers might still notice it was a little rank but would resign themselves to it. It wouldn't be the first time, and she'd compensate with larger portions at the same price. After eight days, old Nestor called on the phone to ask if there was a corpse in the house. Grand Ma had been so annoyed that she was about to explain to him how certain body parts of the living can give off bad smells too, and that he should check out his own home, but changed her mind. The smell was starting to bother her as well.

She boiled the meat inside the bedroom, and we ate of it as much as we could. Tonton and I both got sick. By day twelve, the meat had become crumbly, inedible.

When the gunfire stopped, dead thugs and collateral victims numbered in the dozens. The soldiers were burned or buried. It was rare for a family to claim the remains.

I went two or three times to Bethlehem, with Natacha. There's not much point going there. It's just as poor, smelly and noisy as Divine Power. The fundamental difference is that the homes in Bethlehem are built in ravines and on their banks, ravines in which people dump all their shit. Divine Power is pretty flat, with lots of tiny streams of blackish water in which float plastic bottles of every color, Styrofoam plates, and a variety of non-degradable waste. It was the random hand of poverty that decided whether you scraped by in Bethlehem or in Divine Power, and people moved back and forth all the time. Fany and her sister Élise had lived in Bethlehem originally, but left because they felt threatened by the all-encompassing power of Fanfan le Sauvage, who had learned that Fany was openly badmouthing him.

Fany was convinced that Fanfan was responsible for Pipo's death, that he had left him at the mercy of Franzy Petit Poignet, and was upset that no one was allowed to hold him accountable. It was as if her Pipo, who had been so devoted and so loyal to the gang leader, had never mattered, had never existed. Fany's nightmares, her groans, her orgasmic cries sometimes woke the neighbors, and the teas she drank in the afternoons did nothing to cure her. People said that she and her sister had "the love sickness," and they were among Livio's preferred subjects during vigils.

Moving to Divine Power, for Fany, was like going over to the other side, but no one cared what she thought, and even less so her sister, who never shut up, and whose frenetic prattling about her imaginary lovers exhausted everyone. Freddy just wanted them to settle down. Neither one was an important source of funding, they didn't even have enough to pay the minimum he collected from the residents of Divine Power.

Bethlehem, on the other side of the main avenue, a parody of Jesus's birthplace, as far removed from everything as Divine Power, was just another lost place at the heart of the capital, a boil among others, like Blessed Spring or Hands of Jehovah, from which people averted their eyes but that were so feared, so physically impossible to avoid, that their noises and smells penetrated every nook and cranny of upper- and working-class homes. In order to get to Grand Sud, you had to pass through or by one of these human waste plants and be smacked in the face by the truth that some of us pretended not to know: the inequalities are too stark.

No one could offer a rational explanation for the reciprocal hatred between the cités of Bethlehem and Divine Power. Some played the cynical game of comparison, between levels of degradation, poverty, bravery, gang violence, and the dimensions of women's asses. That last statistic didn't apply to me, though I'd definitely have liked to be more voluptuous once I started "entertaining" to take care of myself and Tonton. There are tons of countries within this one country and I promised myself that one day I'd go see them, get away, even with Tonton on my hands complicating things.

This phone is my link to the world I want. Grand Ma always listened to the radio. The news. Local music. The TV was just for me. Since she left Uncle Frédo and me, I've invented a life on Facebook. I'm "Cécé la Flamme." The name randomly popped into my head. It was just meant to be fun. I said I wanted to burn the place down, that it was the only possible redemption for the slums. My profile picture was a selfie taken close up, my hair pulled back, my mouth painted in a blue lipstick I bought in Martissant. Just my face. I would never show my unattractive body unless I had to. Carlos said that I was skinny, and that being skinny was very good, which makes you wonder why he wasn't. But if I had a body as curvy as Natacha's, I'd for sure be seeing other men besides him. Pierrot used to come by sometimes, too. He'd talk the whole time, dumping whatever was on his mind, his fear of no longer being in Joël's good graces, his broken arm that never properly healed, his agitation. He was a year younger than me and wanted more than anything to prove to me that he was experienced. It was obvious to me that I was his first time, but he still told me about all sorts of women, all kinds of nationalities, that he'd known, all the while stroking the gun he kept near the pillow to impress me. But he didn't hang on me like Carlos who would dare to call me just to tell me how he felt about me. I couldn't maintain that kind of conversation. I never knew what to say. He was too sincere. It was disconcerting. I would imagine his round, clean-shaven, anxious face, his shirt damp because he sweated all the time, and I'd hang up and go back to commenting on what people were posting, even things about which I knew nothing. That's how it was. You just had to respond, to be present, and I desperately needed to exist.

Lots of the people interacting with me on Facebook asked if I was also a gang member. I didn't answer, and if they asked again, I'd unfriend them. There was nothing shocking or brutal about mechanically unfriending someone – friending happened the same way – but it was still serious. We were all playing out our dream lives, which were far more important and real than the ones we lived.

Fire. Fire. For purification, a fresh start. Fire like a threat in the flammable cités. I didn't know how to write very well. People sometimes made fun of me for my mistakes, but everyone made them, in French and in Creole. Whether those years of schooling, despite Grand Ma's efforts, amounted to anything was debatable. I didn't have the impression I knew much more than Soline, who'd dropped out after three years. Impertinence was the main thing, being radical. I didn't believe half of what I posted. I just got lucky. I mostly posted pictures of my feet, food I bought at Morel's, the gullies in the Cité, dead bodies I came across on the street.

Dead bodies did very well. Better than the living. The more sordid or violent the better. Hunger, cholera, measles, or malaria epidemics, people didn't give a shit. Nothing got more attention than a good corpse that was nice and warm or already rotting. The smell went uncaptured.

Joël wanted to see me. He sent Pierrot to fetch me. It was Saturday morning, only ten o'clock, and I was still sleeping. Snoozing at least. It was already very noisy, people going by with buckets of water, laughing, talking loudly. The neighbors' music was loud too, on all sides. Uncle Frédo was snoring. As usual, he'd drunk too much.

Knocking, soft at first, then louder, then very loud. I lifted the pillow I'd put over my head to muffle the noise. It had to be Neighbor Soline, who had been trying to convince me ever since Grand Ma died that she was in charge of me. I got up to open the door, barefoot, my hair a mess, in the tiny blue shorts I wore to bed and a T-shirt – I forget how I came across it – that read in green lettering, *Ministry of the Environment*.

Pierrot was at the door, wearing dark glasses he couldn't have had long because the sticker was still on them, an undershirt with dubious stains – Grand Ma would have been disgusted – an unbuttoned jean shirt, and navy-blue pants with big pockets on the sides like the police wore. It was clear he was packing a gun beneath his shirt.

"What do you want this early?"

"You need to come with me."

"What?"

"The Boss wants to see you. Go change."

"Why does he want to see me? What did I do?"

"No idea. Go get dressed. I have to take you to him." He was serious. I was afraid and I didn't want him to see it. Was Joël going to kill me? I'd heard so many stories about people who were picked up at their homes and never came back. It was assumed that some of the dismembered, burned bodies in the ravine were theirs. Pierrot followed me into the bedroom, afraid I would run away even though the house only had one door. My escape would have meant his death. I took off my shorts, pulled on a pair of jeans, and swapped my top with a white blouse Grand Ma had given me. I needed to look good, these might be the last moments of my life. I'd been embarrassed when I took off my shirt with Pierrot staring at me. He could see my ribs, my tiny breasts. He looked like he had a lump in his throat. I avoided eye contact. I always undressed in the dark for the few customers I had, and most of the time I didn't even bother, just the bottoms.

I could no longer feel my legs. I wanted to see Uncle Frédo, for the last time maybe, but I knew I wouldn't be able to talk to him. I wouldn't even manage to wake him. Pierrot was just as nervous and afraid as I was, and I couldn't tell if it was for himself or for me.

Everyone watched as he escorted me from the house. When Fany saw us, she put her hands on her head as if she were about to cry. It took us ten minutes to walk from my place to "headquarters," a two-story-tall unfinished concrete building, surrounded by high walls built from cinder blocks that hadn't been filled with cement yet, which only gang members were allowed to approach. They must have seen me coming because a man in ragged clothes had already started to slide open the heavy iron gate.

The courtyard was big, with a heavy-duty Toyota parked in front of the unfinished house. The ground was wet around the vehicle, which had clearly just been washed. The second floor was a work-in-progress, just walls in wait of a roof, like all the concrete houses in the Cité. A wide patio faced the courtyard and was furnished with an old cracked-leather office chair and a rocking chair with a yellow cushion. Between the chairs there was a coffee table with cards and dominoes. The cream paint on the walls was chipped in spots. Phone numbers had been written on the walls in ink. A thick white curtain hid the interior from view. I'd have liked to see the room it was hiding and the others too. People used to say that there were cells in the house to hold people who'd been kidnapped and whose families couldn't always be sure of getting them back, even after paying a considerable ransom.

Pierrot told me to wait and headed behind the house. Several men armed with automatic weapons were patrolling the courtyard while others sat on a low wall around a bare tree. Dozens of empty beer bottles and energy-drink cans and used paper plates had been tossed over the wall. The men looked tired. Their button-ups and T-shirts had holes in them from cigarette burns. All of them were as young as Pierrot. One was ripped, with tattoos on his neck and arms; another had dreadlocks down to his waist. A bald, jittery guy kept clearing his throat and spitting. One tall and skinny guy had two guns in his belt and carried an automatic rifle.

No one offered me a seat, so I stood there waiting for forty-five minutes. I was hot, I didn't even have time to wash my face that morning, and my stomach was growling, half from fear, half from hunger.

Suddenly I sensed movement, heard footsteps coming in my direction. Two guys I didn't know, followed by Pierrot, opened the curtain for Joël to come out. Behind his mask of cruelty and a mustache that made him look older than he was, he looked anxious. He had a little belly now. Too much beer, probably.

He sat in the office chair which he gently swiveled. He was wearing a white undershirt under a bulletproof vest, and blue jeans with gray-and-navy Nikes. He took his gun from his belt and set it on the coffee table, knocking off two dominoes, which no one picked up.

"*Sa k pase?*"

"Not too bad," I replied, surprised by the question.

"Cécé la Flamme?"

"Yeah."

He half-shut his eyes and continued to swivel gently in his chair, as if to cradle himself.

"Cécé, do you realize that you've posted a lot more about Fanfan le Sauvage than about me? Is that acceptable behavior for someone living in the Cité of Divine Power? How am I supposed to take that?"

He'd opened his arms wide when he said, "How am I supposed to take that?"

Suddenly I needed to go to the bathroom. I was sweating all over.

"I knew your grandmother well. And I know she would have frowned on this kind of behavior. I mean, you were born here, we're the ones who protect you, who give you lots of privileges. We make it so the young people of this Cité can get by and keep their dignity. Thanks to me, no one can come here and harass folks, and yet you think it's okay to talk more about that mutt than about me?"

I had my arms crossed like I used to whenever Maître Jean-Claude and Madame Sophonie made me recite my lessons. I hadn't even realized that I'd talked more about Fanfan le Sauvage than about Joël.

"I'm sorry. I didn't realize. I was just trying to talk about his protection rackets, how violent he is. . ."

"And you think I'm some sort of choirboy?"

He went silent. I was still standing. It had been over an hour and I was starting to fade. I twisted my hands, which were damp, and I was this close to peeing myself.

Finally he said, "Tell Patience to come here."

The tattooed guy immediately left to fetch Patience. I'd never heard that name before. We waited for five minutes that felt like longer, probably because of the silence. Joël remained calm, looking straight ahead.

Finally, the buff tattooed guy very ceremoniously pulled back the curtain to unveil a beautiful young woman. He was clearly uncomfortable around her. I'd never met anyone who smelled so good. Her perfume filled the whole patio. She was wearing a long, tight, purple strapless dress that showed off her smooth shoulders. She had long extension braids that she kept tucking behind her ears, exposing large hoop earrings. Beautiful flat, sequined sandals showed off toenails painted red. Her fingernails, also painted red, were too long to be real. She had a tiny waist and her ass jiggled under her clingy dress when she walked.

She sat in the rocking chair, without a glance at me or at any of the men who were staring at her in awe. She was focused on herself. You don't see people that glamorous in the Cité. Joël put his right hand on her thigh, which didn't elicit a reaction.

"How many times did she post about that dog from Bethlehem, chérie?"

The *chérie* was deliberate. It sent a message about the nature of their relationship.

"Twenty-three times," replied Patience in a matter-of-fact voice, checking the screen of the latest iPhone in her left hand, as if the phone were supplying the answer. I'd seen pictures of that model online, and it cost more money than I'd ever had in my hands at one time.

"And about me?"

"Three times."

A disapproving murmur rose from the crowd. I didn't know what to say. I was afraid of what might happen to me. Joël started stroking Patience's thigh, again to total indifference. In a stern voice, he said,

"You're gonna fix this. You're gonna talk about me. You're no longer allowed to post about that moron from Bethlehem, except to put him down. Pierrot and Cassave will periodically give you updates on all the good things we're doing for the people in the Cité of Divine Power."

"Okay," I said.

The tall skinny guy took three steps forward when Joël said his name, Cassave, which he's surely been given because of how skinny he was. Joël took his weapon from the table, dislodging some more dominoes. Everyone moved back. Getting up, he stirred the cloud of Patience's perfume. She kept looking at her phone.

"Follow me, Patience," Joël said, passing through the curtain as the bald man held it open.

I looked at Cassave, Pierrot, then the muscular tattooed guy, who motioned to me with his left hand, the rifle in his right. The same man who'd let me in opened the gate again for me to leave, but just a crack, as if he had noted the exact space required by my tiny body to leave the headquarters.

The way back was long. More than ten minutes walking under a brutal sun. I wasn't moving as quickly as on the way there, I was too hungry, too thirsty. I was thinking about the bread that I dunked every morning into the sweetened coffee I bought from the ladies at the end of the street. It was too late for my bread and coffee, better to go straight for lunch, a large plate of rice and mashed peas, topped with eggplant. I'd have some left over for Tonton. Once I ate, I'd reflect on my surreal morning.

Curious neighbors were looking at me. The entire Cité was aware that I'd been summoned by the Boss. Fany and Élise, almost hidden behind the big pots in which Fany grew her plants, signaled for me to come over when they saw me. They were afraid. I pretended not to see them. Old Nestor was standing in the middle of the alleyway as if to bar my way, but I split off towards Edner's, the shortest way to get something to eat, hoping he'd be gone on my way back. I'd worn the same jeans the day before, and had two five-hundred-gourde bills in my right pocket. I felt like I wasn't allowed to say anything about what had just happened.

When I got home, I closed the door. Soline came knocking around three o'clock in the afternoon. Someone must have called to tell her about my summons, and she'd judged it important enough to leave her spice stand and come check on me, in honor of her friendship with Grand Ma. I didn't open. The phone was turned off next to me on the bed. I was realizing that it was good to disconnect sometimes. I thought about Patience, about her perfume, her beauty, her detachment. I fell asleep.

The shutters didn't let in much light and so the bedroom was never very bright, which was useful if I wanted to nap during the day.

I must have slept a long time. I woke up wondering what time it could be. I stared at the ceiling, which I found calming. The gray sheet metal, the light wooden slats overrun by termites all the way to the walls. It was six in the evening and mass had just started in the three closest churches. It was easy to pick out Victor's voice promising hellfire and unspeakable retributions for those who did not follow God's commandments.

At first, it was a light scratching. Could have been anything. Someone passing by, one of the many stray dogs in the Cité. The wind. No. Someone had knocked. It couldn't be Tonton, he had a key, and managed to open the door even when he was completely wasted.

Twice. Three times. Five times.

"It's me…"

It had to be six thirty.

"Go away! Not today."

"Please open. I need to talk to you. On Facebook they're saying you got beat up by Joël's men."

I got up and opened the door. Carlos' large silhouette absorbed what remained of daylight. This time, he was wearing a pair of jeans with his striped shirt, but it didn't suit him any better.

It was completely dark now in the room. The electricity was out, and I didn't have any matches to light the kerosene lamp. Carlos took a lighter from his pocket which he put to the wick until a small, sad flame sprang up. He placed the slightly blackened glass delicately on the lamp's collar. I lay back on the bed without saying anything, and he sat on the slightly-rusted iron chair beside it.

"What happened?"

"I don't want to talk about it. I can't talk about it."

"They're saying online that they made you go there and abused you."
"No one abused me."
"I was worried."

I turned on my phone. A blue glow came out. I had dozens of messages and just as many friend requests, including one from Patience. In her profile photo, her hair framed her entire face and she was wearing large glasses. She had on blood-red lipstick that contrasted with the black rim of her glasses and her dark hair. All of a sudden, I could smell her perfume in the room and I shivered. Joël had probably asked her to keep an eye on me.

"You're shaking. Have you eaten?"
"Everything's fine, thanks," I answered curtly.

I was always harsh with Carlos. I didn't know why, since he was actually really nice to me, and was the only person who showed he cared.

He started stroking my hair. I let him, reluctantly. I think I was just uncomfortable with any sign of affection. Grand Ma had really loved me, but we didn't have a tactile relationship. She never took me in her arms or stroked my hair. I'd have liked to explain to Carlos that our relationship wasn't what he imagined, that I saw someone else who also paid me, and that, if I could, I'd see as many men as possible, that it was the only way I'd found to avoid begging in the street or selling random knick-knacks that wouldn't bring in enough money to feed Tonton and me.

There were tons of comments. Some were saying I'd been killed and my body tossed into a ravine and burned. Others were demanding that the police open an investigation, and that the government commissioner assume responsibility. People had been calling in to the radio stations all day to denounce the gangs, government laxity, etc. A woman had interjected on behalf of Joël's gang to say that I was just fine and like all the residents of the Cité, protected by the Boss himself. She received a torrent of insults in response. It was a big noisy mess, and I was at the center of it. I had to post something to put an end to the debate, find a way to say that I was alive. As lively as a controversy can seem on social networks, it fades fast. Another story would overtake mine unless I fired back to keep it going. So I wrote as Carlos watched, intrigued: "Boss Joël wants to protect our Cité."

I turned off my phone again, taking flight before the deluge of hateful comments. I wanted Carlos to leave. I wanted to rinse myself off behind the house, which I hadn't been able to that day, and even though there was only a gallon of water left since I hadn't gone to get any in three days.

"I'm thinking of leaving the Cité. I'm building a house in Tabarre. The gangs there aren't as violent and it's easier to run a business. I'm moving my drinks shop and I want you to come with me. We could work together, get stuff done. I think you're really in danger in the Cité, even if you refuse to talk about what happened this morning."

"Nothing happened this morning. I want you to go now. I have a headache."

The chair squeaked when Carlos got up. He stood for a minute or two, waiting maybe for me to say something. He gently pushed the door open to leave. I got up and locked it, which made no sense since, just as soon as I had, I took my towel and the gallon of water to go and wash myself.

Thing is you had to go fetch the water. Far sometimes. Mimose, then Lana, used to take care of it. Grand Ma would let me go with them sometimes, gallon jug in hand. Some days it was a whole trek to find some. I remember long exhausting walks in the sun, the debates that went on and on until finally a group assembled to share a tip, or an address where buying a bucket got you a gallon. Those outings must have been respites for the women, men, children and teenagers who, like Mimose and Lana, helped out people barely less impoverished than they were. They got to escape, temporarily, from very hard work and, in the case of the children and teens, abuse. Some of the married women, who had several kids, who were miserable and tormented and unable to meet the daily household needs, not to mention those of a husband who they'd been taught was the head of the family, which meant nothing in practice, took advantage of the water runs to chat, never really lingering on their hardships, out of reserve, but also because they were hopeful that their lives would improve.

The sale of water was an important business in the Cité. You had to be resourceful to live here, invent a job for yourself, even if it was breaking rocks to sell the pieces to anyone with the means to build a real house. Several residents had made cisterns that they filled using trucks. Sometimes we waited a long time for one of those big-bellied vehicles to deliver water. Whichever cistern owner had the most clout with gang leaders would get supplied whenever things heated up, and the Cité started making the front page for the shoot-outs and the casualties, and the whole time the politicians and anyone who wanted to become one gave radio interviews on life in the slums that most of them had never visited. The precious element would become more expensive, even doubling in price. You'd have to grease the palms of several middlemen who delivered it from the *patron* or *patronne* to the dealers. All forms of violence were fair game in these precarious places.

Grand Ma also wasn't above resorting to hiring Livio to be her "waterboy," as she put it. He was always happy to make a little money. He didn't get paid when he emceed at vigils, where he told stories so dirty that certain God-fearing women would inquire to find out if he'd be there or not before deciding to attend. The crown of Livio's head was forever mussed from all the heavy containers of water he carried on his head. He'd walk fast in his ripped clothes and tan plastic shoes, smiling at lord knows who or what, maybe jokes he was making up as he went in anticipation of the next vigil.

I continued to call on him for this thankless chore. Tonton and I didn't need much water, just enough to wash once a day, and do a little laundry every so often. Livio would fill the big blue plastic container in the corner of the room as needed. And the gallon jugs too, set aside after Ma had used up the oil or vinegar they contained. We'd had about fifty of them before Grand Ma died, taking up the whole bedroom, and I gave them away, to Soline mostly, to old Nestor, and to Fany, so now there were ten left.

The water was always lukewarm, no matter the time of day or night you used it. The roof of the house was low, the sun always beating down, plus the constant buzz of the Cité must have had something to do with it too, I told myself. Carlos told me I shouldn't drink that water, gathered from rivers, transported by truck, poured into cisterns that were never washed, where it then sat for several days. But Grand Ma drank that water her whole life, and so have I, and nothing ever happened to us, or at least we never connected our diarrhea or fever to the water we consumed. Still, I took his advice, and started buying little bags of water or bottles. I couldn't imagine ever drinking the water Livio delivered again. I also understood why the Cité was carpeted with those muddied bags and never-ending plastic bottles of every color that were also used to sell energy drinks, sodas and juices.

Carlos tried to show me what ugliness was. He was always talking about the environment and natural disasters. The earthquake in 2010 was only the beginning, according to him. I didn't pay much attention when he went on one of his long, know-it-all rants, but I couldn't stop myself from looking over at him when he mentioned disasters worse than the last earthquake. Which simply wasn't possible. I'd still been a kid but I remember the dead bodies, the screams of pain and hopelessness, the mayhem.

"There's nothing here for you, come with me," he said all in one breath as he tried to grab the hand I was hurriedly shoving in my jeans pocket.

I didn't answer. I'd stopped reacting so that he'd understand he had to leave. More and more often I'd make sure not to be home at six, or to pretend like I wasn't and not answer the door. I hadn't been the same person since I got summoned to see Joël. Neither was he. He seemed even more afraid than I was. I preferred Tonton's impassibility. His way of having nothing but his body to drag around, to quench and rest, was fascinating. Carlos seemed contemptuous of Tonton, always staring at him with suspicion. Which bothered and annoyed me. His protective side wasn't welcome. I wasn't looking for a dad.

There had to be other men in the Cité or nearby who didn't mind paying for a distraction. So why did I have to put up with this fat man who wanted to control me and take me away from the only family I had? Grand Ma had it right when she said we all need a family.

I loved the rain. Too bad it came with so much inconvenience. The roof of the house was so rotten and riddled with holes that I had to set out containers to capture the water that fell on the bed, the table, the floor, everywhere. When I was little, I used to go outside and bathe in the rain, and now I took great pleasure in watching kids gleefully run, clothed or naked, under the raindrops, and at how people bustled to collect it, though the water will never be enough to clean up the muck and filth the rain brings into homes made of cardboard, plastic, and recycled sheet metal, the roads flooded, the main avenue impassable, even for cars.

When it rained, no one went outside. Carlos didn't come. All that water worried people, kept them apart. There was so much waste and stench among the residents of the lower part of town that they became more uncivil than usual. The slightest sideways look could trigger deadly brawls and start cycles of vengeance capable of lasting for months. All these messes must have contributed somehow to the widespread indifference.

It must have been nine in the evening, a Friday. People didn't go to bed early in the Cité. Uncle Frédo hadn't come home yet. Was he ever really home? Did he even know who I was? I had my doubts, which were on occasion erased by his faint smile. I would put leftovers for him on Styrofoam plates on his little iron bed. He'd eat without looking at his meal, maybe without even knowing what it was. He was drunk and it was dark. There was no light in his tiny room. No need. That night I'd left him some pork and fried bananas. The bananas were probably cold and stiff, but he wouldn't care. I was lying on my back, in the light of the kerosene lamp, fooling around on my phone. I had three thousand nine hundred and seventeen friends on Facebook. The number went up as I posted photos and commented on random subjects and situations however I could, and wanted, with all the malice I could muster. I now had a Facebook page for Cécé la Flamme; I could tell I was going to soon pass the number of friends allowed by the network. I posted photos and comments directly on the page, and invited my contacts to visit and read them.

The beautiful and buxom Patience whom I so envied had posted nothing in several days. I'd accepted her friendship, and she liked all my posts, even the photos of Élise's pathetic plant in a sad half-broken pot on cracked earth that testified better than anything else to the heat and the rain that hadn't fallen in seven weeks. She was keeping an eye on me, for sure.

At nine in the evening, Mass was over, the churchgoers were home, and radios were on full blast. Someone knocked violently on the door.

"Who is it?" I asked angrily. I had the same tone as Grand Ma, I missed her so much.

It had to be Carlos, and I was going to forbid him to ever come to my house after six in the evening. I yanked open the door to find myself face to face with Pierrot and the tall, lanky guy whom I'd last seen armed to the teeth, the one Joël had called Cassave.

"Do you need something? Cause I'm not selling anything!"

Clearly I had my Grand Ma's energy tonight.

They seemed taken aback by my reaction.

"Sorry," said the tall, skinny one, turning around, like he wanted to leave.

"No, it's just I wanted to see you, and Jules here agreed to come with me... I wanted to buy you a beer and tell you I'm sorry for the last time," Pierrot stammered. "Morel's is pretty lit tonight..."

Jules still had his back turned. I told them to wait so I could throw my sneakers on.

Morel's was a hip place. You could eat there any night of the week, but on the weekends lots of Cité gang members went there to grab a beer or drink some rum. Morel was less jovial than when I'd been there last with Carlos. You could tell he was embarrassed by the heavily armed clientele. He seemed older and balder than the last time, and he pretended not to recognize me. He understood the price of silence and talk in the Cité. We sat around one of the white plastic tables. Beers arrived right away. I hadn't noticed Jules or Pierrot ordering them. They must have been regulars. The beer was the local brand, served frosted. All three of us had our cell phones out as if we were alone. And we were, in fact. I had no desire to be in their company.

It was Jules who broke the silence by asking my name.

"Célia Jérôme. Cécé."

"Jules César."

Jules César was a little older than Pierrot and me. By four or five years. He'd done two years of college. He'd studied Social Communication until, overcome by rage, he'd killed the owner of the little room he shared with his mom in Delmas 19. The bastard was always harassing them – he'd said, running his right hand across his face – for rent money they didn't have. His poor mom, who'd died from respiratory failure at the age of forty-eight, used to sell, depending on the season, mangoes, grilled corn, or Spanish limes by the side of the road. She didn't earn enough, but she insisted that he stay in school. That moneygrubber would come knocking at all hours of the day and night, subjecting the poor woman to nasty threats and cursing her out.

He told me very matter-of-factly how, on that day in May, he'd been lying on the floor mattress he shared with his mom, reading Jacques Attali's *Karl Marx or the Spirit of the World*, when he heard that piece of shit insult the poor woman as she cried. Impossible to keep his mind on the page. He really lost it when the man told his mother that she was still young and that instead of selling rotten mangoes that didn't bring in enough to cover the rent and support her lazy prick of a son, whose ambitions far exceeded his means, she'd be better off selling her fat ass. He gave a nasty laugh, pleased that this last indignity had elicited the same reaction from the neighbors who'd come out of their makeshift homes to watch. Jules César, not realizing what he was doing, grabbed the pink two-kilo barbells with which he worked out every morning in a futile attempt to build some arm muscle – they were the only things handy in the poorly-furnished room – and used them to bash in the bastard's head until nothing remained but a mash of blood, bone, and brain. Some of the neighbors tried to hold him back, but he turned on them and they ran away. His mother couldn't stop screaming. When he came back to his senses, he saw her frail silhouette outlined as if in a fog, and that was the last time he saw her, standing five foot four, next to his six three. Amid the chaos, he'd heard the words "police" and "justice of the peace," and took off like a madman, barefoot, in just his shorts and a blood-stained undershirt. He caught his breath on Avenue Christophe. Without realizing, he'd taken the route he took to get to college every day. Luckily, the sun was going down. He walked to Boulevard Jean-Jacques Dessalines, thinking he'd find his friend Clovis, who lived in Bethlehem. But he didn't have his cell phone, and wasn't sure he could find Clovis's place in the maze of the Cité.

"It was God," he added, after a gulp of beer. "He guided me, and I went straight there. It was the door. I'd noticed it the one time Clovis had me over. A carved door, taken from some fancy house, probably during a *déchoukaj*."

"I knocked. Clovis opened, not all that surprised to see me. He lent me an old shirt, a pair of pants and rubber sandals. But he didn't have room to put me up. 'See you tomorrow,' he'd said, like he expected to see me at school. But school was over for me. I walked until I got to the Cité of Divine Power. I needed to be in a neighborhood where honest police don't enter. It was already 10 P.M. Freddy's guys stopped me. They brought me to the Boss. God was with me all the way. They could have killed me. The Boss asked me if Fanfan le Sauvage had sent me to spy on him. I told him the whole story. He liked the way I talked. He asked if I could write well too. He let me sleep on a flattened cardboard box in the courtyard. I was the only one without a weapon.

The next day, all the radio stations were talking about what I did. They also said that my mother, in a state of shock, had been admitted to the General Hospital, until she could be cross-examined. The guys in the gang started showing me some respect. I was being talked about in the media, just like the Boss. I was afraid but nobody needed to know that. Your first murder changes lots of things in your life. And then the rest comes almost naturally. You have no choice. You're in it. You're a little more afraid of dying yourself. It's just so quick, overwhelming actually, when you see a person, in the span of a few seconds, lose their balance, go from vertical to horizontal, without any chance of ever getting back up. I feel up my different weapons a few times a day. I like weapons. Their destructive power. I'm sure I'll die by bullet. But lots of folks will die before me. They'll say hello to Guerda for me."

I started and opened my eyes, sure I had missed part of his story. I was getting really tired, it was almost midnight, and the only people left were a couple not talking to each other at a table in the corner. The man was well into his sixties. The girl couldn't have been older than seventeen. She was drinking Coca-Cola, and him, rum.

"Guerda was *ma petite maman*."

He must have been on his tenth beer. Mine was a warm liquid by then, and I'd only drunk a quarter of it. Typically, my limit was one. Pierrot had moved closer to an electrical outlet so he could charge his cell phone and surf Facebook, laughing to himself. Morel had just brought two more beers to Jules César who let out a belch by way of thank you. He really had no shame.

"Maman died in the public hospital. Alone. Like some nobody. All she had was me. All I had was her. Neighbor Justine went to see her twice. But she was old, her feet were always swollen. The second visit, she'd waited a week, Justine found someone else in my mom's bed. She asked the doctors and nurses, who weren't much help, if she'd been transferred or had left. In the end, the patient in the next bed told Justine my mom had died."

Jules César emptied his eleventh beer in one go. I didn't feel like listening to him talk about his mom any more, or justifying why he was a criminal. I was sure he'd killed more than one person since his neighbor. Now he had the hiccups and was burping shamelessly without excusing himself. Clearly he hadn't read that that was bad manners in his book about the spirit of the world or whatever. He had started into his twelfth beer, taking small swigs, when he suddenly asked me:

"Can I spend the night with you?"

"No!"

The no came out by itself. Yeah, I was looking for customers, but this wasted, burping, blabbermouth – plus he was a criminal! – was too much. I figured he might be too tall to fit in the house anyway. No way.

I was mad at Pierrot for leaving me alone with this Jules César who so desperately needed to tell his life story. Obviously he was looking for a mother. It wouldn't be me.

Pierrot settled the bill, pulling out a wad of gourdes that Morel eyed enviously. Me too. The boys walked me home. Jules César had a gun in each hand. Pierrot carried one in his left. He hadn't used his right arm since Freddy had broken it, but he never talked about it. I walked in the middle. It was a beautiful night. The alleys smelled of rot and were deserted, apart from two male dogs that both wanted to mount a female and seemed about to fight. Pierrot put his gun back in his belt and tried to grab my hand, but I put it in my pocket to show him that I wasn't interested. Good thing, I was thinking, that none of the neighbors were awake to see me with Pierrot and Jules César, except I knew that Élise was huddled behind the wall of her patio. She didn't dare show her face but I could smell her cigarette. Tomorrow, lots of people would know that I'd come home escorted by members of Joël's gang.

Patience was a First Lady, just like the president's wife. She had a flock of people at her service who tried to guess her wants, feared falling out of favor, and who begged her to intervene on their behalf before the Boss. She wore long, elegant dresses and cloaked herself in mystery, and there was only one thing you needed to know about her and could talk about it in all serenity: she was the Boss's girlfriend. She had no known past.

Patience wanted the women to get organized. To understand their importance and their role in the Cité's development. She decided to gather them all together. Pierrot was tasked with delivering invitations to the most "valiant" to a meeting that would be held on Thursday morning. It was more of a summons laced with threats than an invitation.

"The Boss's girl expects you on Thursday at 9:30 A.M. for a meeting."

"About what?"

"How should I know? Just make sure you're there. She doesn't like it when people are late. Don't say I didn't warn you."

I rarely woke before ten, but that day I was up and washed, hair done, by eight, wearing my regular jeans and the same white blouse I'd worn when Joël summoned me. It was the most presentable outfit I owned. I sat on the edge of the bed. I wasn't hungry. I didn't want to be on my phone. I was wondering what I'd done, or not done, this time. I gave myself thirty minutes to get to headquarters, even though it was ten minutes away.

I'd been waiting for fifteen minutes when Soline arrived. She'd gotten even fatter and walked with her legs apart because of her weight. Then Andrise, the pastor's wife, who was definitely going to be hot in her purple velvet jacket. She was always trying to show how proper she was, which ended up making her look weird, comical if you ask me. The velvet jacket was doing that right now, and I wanted to take a photo but didn't dare. Yvrose looked tired – I'd heard that Fénelon was sick. Her bulging eyes made her head look even bigger than normal. Fany had gone all out, ironic for someone too busy nursing her grief to go anywhere. She was wearing a pretty dress in a dusky pink color, with silver flats, and she'd straightened her hair. She even had a little leather bag over her shoulder. It was a big-day outfit.

The gate slid open for us to enter, a little wider than it had for me the last time. You had to take into account the volume of some of those bodies passing through. The big SUV was gone. A tent had been set up and chairs arranged beneath it. We took our spots. Other women had already arrived. Maybe ten. Natacha was one of them. I'd never seen her skin so dewy. She was a little younger than me and already had two kids. She was sweating heavily and sponging her face with tissues that left little bits on her brow and cheeks. She was seated across from me, and we exchanged a smile.

I'd seen all the other women before. They were vendors and homemakers, like Joe's and Edner's wives. Maybe they were valiant. What did I know? I certainly wasn't, even if I had no intention of saying that to Patience.

She joined us at 9:45, preceded by her perfume and followed by the tattooed guy carrying a machine gun. When she got to the middle of the gathering, she said hello and turned to see everyone. She started to talk to us the way you'd talk to very young children, dragging out each word, afraid we wouldn't understand. If only I could have filmed her, I kept thinking, and made everyone laugh the way I felt like doing as she talked. But everyone would have known it was me. The other women had phones like Grand Ma's, except for Natacha, but no one would have suspected her. Everyone's attention would turn to Cécé la Flamme, and they'd find my charred body in one of the alleys. A fat drop of sweat slid down my back.

"Ladies, you are the *potomitans* of the Cité. Boss Joël is trying very hard to bring prices down so you can feed your families without hardship, and he wants to be able to count on you so we can live in peace. He needs your support to accomplish his mission, and you should talk to your husbands to make sure they are devoted to him too. He's here to protect us all."

It was getting hot. And the beautiful Miss Patience's idiotic spiel wasn't helping. The other women watched her in astonishment, without a word. Soline had wrinkles across her forehead. The thug with dreadlocks showed up carrying a stainless-steel tray with plastic glasses of Coca-Cola, Sprite, and Cola Couronne. Thankfully I was in front and could grab one of the Cola Couronnes, the local sugary soda most people liked. It was cold, with ice cubes. I heard Patience's voice as if from afar, because the fried patties arrived right after the drinks on a similar tray carried by the jittery bald guy. I hoped he hadn't spit on them, because I helped myself to two, I was so hungry. And I'd have liked to take a third back to Uncle Frédo.

The tray went back completely empty; clearly I wasn't the only one to take two. Lots of the ladies had crumbs around their mouths, so I used the front camera of my phone to make sure I didn't.

"The Boss cares about you and your families and has gifts for all of you that he's sure you'll like. Ladies, you are our mothers, our sisters, our friends, you are the pillars of our community."

The dreadlocks guy and the jittery guy then placed a half-filled bag in front of each of us. I could guess what it held. It was rice from the cargo seized three days ago on Harry Truman Boulevard. Photos of the operation had circulated on Facebook, and I'd recognized Joël himself, Pierrot, Jules César, and the nervous spitter.

"There'll be another get-together soon and we will continue the battle for our Cité, and our country."

I would love to have known what battle Patience was talking about, I hadn't heard of any. Neither had the other ladies, who looked at each other in confusion. They certainly had nothing in common with this woman who lived surrounded by armed men, didn't need to work, and had everything she wanted and then some. Still, they were pleased with the unexpected sack of rice, which they would valiantly eat or sell, or both.

I wasn't much of a cook though, so I planned to have Soline sell my half-sack for me. It was easier that way, less tiring, and more cost-effective for me to buy from other sellers, who were incidentally generous with their servings to me because of Grand Ma.

There were fifteen very respectful *au revoir madame*s in a row, to which Patience idiotically replied, "Au revoir, chérie," without any feeling, disembodied almost, with a smile that lasted too long to be sincere. Her beauty and her curvaceous figure complimented by her tight, white dress were of no use to her in this moment. And she probably sensed it.

The sack weighed a ton, and I'd gladly have paid Livio to carry it for me, but he wasn't around, and there was no question of leaving it and coming back later. The other women seemed to have less trouble. They were taller and better built. I had to switch arms every two minutes to make it back to the house.

I'd already seen lots of dead bodies in my life. Whole ones. Dismembered ones. Charred ones. Grand Ma's. I'd keep on my way past the bodies, mostly men's, laid out in the sun, attracting flies, starving dogs, living Christians. Ma used to say I had dry eyes. That I didn't know how to cry. It was true. And yet some days I'd have liked to, because there was nothing easier and no doubt more liberating. Letting yourself go, so then other people console you or make a fuss over you. For being weak, for daring to suffer a little more than them, and showing it.

Fénelon was sick. I'd heard a couple of people talking about it. Soline was helping Yvrose as best she could, like lots of women in the neighborhood. She asked me to pitch in too, since I didn't have much to do during the day, so that she could keep her shop open. She wouldn't have understood if I'd explained that social media takes time, that you had to look at lots of photos, like them or not, comment on what was going on in politics or with artists in the HMI – god I loved pronouncing those three letters, in English if you please!, haitch-em-eye, which stood for Haitian Music Industry. Plus I had to occasionally sing the praises of our all-powerful and generous leader, Joël. I had posted a photo of the sacks of rice Patience had given us on Facebook. She liked my post right away, and commented: "It's only the beginning. Once school's back in session, Boss Joël will make sure that every student in the Cité of Divine Power receives a hot meal daily."

The government commissioner himself went on the radio to remind people that anyone who received stolen merchandise was an accomplice of the thieves. He was widely berated on the internet.

I was getting more and more followers on my Facebook page, which was becoming easier to manage. I didn't even have to unfriend the haters anymore, meaning anyone who went too far, lectured me, or tried to get me to rat out the criminals in Joël's gang.

I agreed to help Yvrose. Her two sons were working in the Dominican Republic. I vaguely remembered two dull, pimply boys who looked a lot alike, had similar names, Jean-Pierre and Jean-Paul, and wore the same shirts as if it was too much trouble for their parents to pick out different fabrics. They were forever explaining to anyone who called them twins that they were, in fact, not, that there were three years between them. No one cared.

Fénelon and Yvrose's shop was the front room of their home. On the wall, in red paint, was written: L'ETERNEL EST GRAND. Most of the time, it was Fénelon behind the counter. He always tried to hit on the women who came in for their groceries, offering them credit and little gifts in exchange for sexual favors. His wife was aware of this, and more than a few times had gone to ask his presumed mistresses to pay up, often getting a volley of rocks thrown at her in return. The neighbors would say she was so skinny because her constant jealousy kept her from sleeping and eating.

Yvrose motioned for me to come in around the back when she saw me. I went down a short and very narrow alleyway that led to a wooden door. A young woman was leaning against the wall, staring at the ground. I said hello. She didn't answer, maybe I hadn't spoken loud enough. I pulled aside a white lace curtain that led into the couple's bedroom. The bed Fénelon was in was big, and the pink blanket that covered him – embroidered around the edges – was pretty. The room was cluttered but clean. The massive bed: a large wooden bureau with drawers below and shelves up top that held little porcelain cats, dogs, birds, and big shells, plus three carved wooden chairs with the same designs as the bed's headboard. The bedroom adjoined the shop, and Yvrose came in through a door I hadn't noticed, whose squeaking woke her husband.

Fénelon looked around, his mouth half-open. He was wearing a white undershirt, and the rest of his body was covered by a white sheet. He closed his eyes again.

Yvrose whispered that he'd had a stroke, that his left side was paralyzed, and he could no longer speak, that he needed help with everything, which was exhausting, that she'd hired Manita to cook and clean, but that she still needed help to be able to run her business which was the couple's only source of income and even let them send a little bit to their sons who weren't doing that well.

Fénelon woke up again. It was likely the pots banging in the courtyard; Manita, who must have been the girl I'd seen in the alley, was making food or doing dishes, probably both. Suddenly there was a terrible smell. Fénelon had gotten extremely agitated when he saw me. Yvrose removed an adult diaper from a pack under the bed. Fénelon complained, looking at his wife, then me. He clearly didn't want me to stay.

"I think he doesn't want you to see me change his diaper, Cécé. You get it. You're a young woman, and he's a man..."

I had no desire to watch either. It would have been the second time I'd seen him completely vulnerable. Apparently he hadn't forgotten our little romp and how it had ended for him. Me seeing him get his ass wiped like a baby would have done him in altogether.

I had no pity for him though. I'd thought about Mimose and felt ashamed. Why had I tattled on her? Because I was that angry about a cola? She'd never hurt me. I reminded myself that I had been just a kid but I didn't feel any better. I understood now what it meant to have no money, to be hungry or afraid of running out of food.

Fénelon won't be buying any more women's favors. Soline had told me he would be paralyzed for life. Yvrose will have no more reasons to be jealous. She'll change his diapers, bring him food, work like hell to keep the store running, and stop worrying about his absences. On the way back to my place, I thought I could smell competing odors of mint and shit.

It was my birthday. Not that I had any connection to time. Time didn't really pass in Bethlehem or the Cité of Divine Power. Probably everywhere where people don't expect anything. We forgot to exist, and didn't bother trying to understand. But I felt like saying something about it to Uncle Frédo. Did he even know what a birthday was? What was his? He didn't have any ID, actually. He'd come back from his America like an errant package: return to sender.

Ma had always remembered my birthday. When I was little, she would give me a bit of money that I'd put in my homemade piggybank, a jar with a slot in the lid. The money would disappear at some point. She'd take it back when she needed some, promising to pay it back. And she would give me money throughout the year, but it didn't add up to the same. When I dared bring it up, she would look at me, feigning astonishment, and say: "What money, *petite*?" I didn't blame her. As a teenager, I started to spend the money before she could take it back and, since I loved beauty products, I'd buy myself bargain lipsticks, powders that didn't match my complexion, dark blue eye-shadow, and yellow, green, or black nail polish. Ma laughed herself to tears when she saw me, calling my makeup some sort of Kanaval get-up. She said nail polish was supposed to be red or pink. I'd get upset and she'd laugh even harder.

Tonton sometimes slept till three in the afternoon. Once he was awake, he'd stay in bed staring at the ceiling, waiting for the Angelus before going out. He wouldn't say anything, or ask for anything. I brought him something to eat and stayed a while looking at him. He had trouble with plastic forks. They're too soft. Grand Ma had left me plates and silverware I could have used, but that would have required me to wash them afterwards, and at his age, Tonton wasn't going to suddenly understand he needed to help with the housework.

Carlos would have made a big deal if I told him that I'd turned twenty-two. He would have taken it as me softening up, almost an acceptance of his suggestion that I go live with him in Tabarre. He used to talk about how the construction on his house was going, two stories of concrete, and the entire ground floor reserved for storage and selling his drinks. It was obvious money wouldn't be a problem. In a couple of years, I'd probably be like Yvrose, a bit tight-lipped, ageless, with a big head that bobbled when I walked.

I didn't say anything. I let him dream alone. I couldn't chase him away. My life and Tonton's depended on it. He was the only one I saw. I wouldn't open the door for Pierrot anymore. He scared me. The last time, he had shown up drunk, with Jules César who was equally wasted.

I told them to get lost. I was really afraid. Luckily, Élise and Livio were at home, and Soline was on her porch. The boys took their nonsense elsewhere, guns in hand. Afterwards, I sent a WhatsApp message to Pierrot, telling him not to bother me anymore. He read the message but didn't respond.

I caught myself waiting. I don't know what I was looking forward to more, Carlos or the money he gave me. 6:30 P.M. Tonton left. Carlos came in. They didn't greet each other. Tonton because he didn't see or hear anyone, because he was irrevocably pulled toward the earth, slumped over, carrying his memories and what little future he had. Carlos because he was stiff, wrapped up in his ideas of work, success, and proper behavior, which led him to look down on gang members, alcoholics, homosexuals, and whores. It was this blindness, this lack of humanity, this pride, this arrogance that led him to think of me as his girlfriend. He was wrong. My intentions had always been crystal clear. I'd made the choice to support myself. True, I hadn't had much success thus far, I didn't have the body for the job, and the competition was tough, but I couldn't think of him as anything but a customer. Before he left my house, he had to give me a thousand gourdes. I was actually thinking of raising the price.

Carlos liked to think he had a normal life, in a normal world. He would tell me about his mother, a woman who knew how to read and write, who had gone to Catholic school, whose life had taken bad turns, who found herself alone with four children from four different fathers, who had moved heaven and earth to get them a proper education. A good woman!

Carlos must have desperately hoped that I'd be like that saint he was so eager for me to meet. He was thirty-six and still living with her, so of course he wanted to show her that he had someone in his life. But what will she say when she finds out that not only am I not in her son's life, but that I'm one of those people who don't even believe in their own existence? Maybe because of the impossibility of a future, that inability to have a hand in your own destiny, to get to the end of something that has meaning for you and others.

The shriek echoed in the middle of the night. A woman's shriek. Sharp. It was harder to ignore than the sound of gunfire. Victims of gang battles were buried in secret, their parents either too ashamed or too afraid of crossing the victors. This nocturnal scream announced a death for which the family had the right to mourn. It came from nearby. Other sounds, other cries of pain, other voices, of women and men, joined that first cry.

Fénelon had left us. He died in his sleep. Soline told me he'd stopped eating. He'd been kept alive a few days thanks to an IV drip, and his wife was exhausted from watching over him day and night.

It was six in the morning when I went outside to see what was going on. Frédo hadn't heard anything. Even an earthquake like the one in 2010 wouldn't have roused him. I was among the last to arrive. I had trouble squeezing into the room there were so many people. Soline gave me a look filled with reproach and anger. It was my late arrival plus my pink top, not the appropriate color in a house in mourning. She must have gotten there right away, at the first cry, with her bottle of olive oil and her coarse salt treatment for emotional upheaval. She seemed tired, and her nightgown peeked out under her brown and beige dress. Everyone gathered around Yvrose, who was sitting in one of the three chairs in the bedroom, Andrise to her right, Fany her left, weeping and every so often letting out a long strident cry. An exemplary husband, she proclaimed him, a model of human virtue. The neighbors in the room took turns adding a new layer to the sanctity of the departed. I had nothing to say. The body hadn't been taken away yet. It was covered with a white sheet.

Kick the bucket and just like that, all the bad things you did get erased? Everyone in the room, or nearly, knew how Fénelon had behaved around women and girls. The body beneath the sheet was no longer the man who had jammed his fingers into my vagina so violently that I was sore for a week, who had sobbed over his lost prowess in my presence, hoping perhaps that I would console him. It was a lump of flesh that would begin decomposition soon, and for a long time, his loved ones would think they heard his voice, think him not far off, that he'll open the door and walk into the house, bringing with him the outside, the unknown, the bad and the good thoughts.

The ornamental cats, dogs, and fish sympathetically watched the comings and goings, the sad faces. Good thing they were there, their faces didn't change, even before death itself.

Patience visited Yvrose in the afternoon. A vague commotion preceded her, a rumor, armed scouts, sketchy, unidentifiable men running in every direction, people out on their stoops to catch a glimpse of the strange creature who left a trail of perfume in her wake, and who supposedly made the Boss and some of his men lose their minds. Earlier in the day she had posted a message of condolence for Yvrose, a member of the group of valiant women of the Cité and steadfast supporter of the revered Boss, who was devastated by the death of her husband, a no-less-steadfast supporter of the much-loved Boss. I "liked" her post. I was being sincere. Her audacity amazed me.

She was wearing a long, figure-hugging black dress, a long necklace of white pearls that came down to her belly button, and large black glasses that made her red mouth pop. Her black braids fell all the way to the small of her back, and you could tell it wasn't the plastic hair girls in the Cité wore.

Yvrose had been given the heads-up and was waiting in front of the house. It was quite a show. She had on a white dress and a headscarf in the same color. Patience took her in her arms as the neighbors watched, moved. The whole thing was so put on, and so badly, that I almost burst out laughing. They went into the house. Manita, the young woman Yvrose had hired, was the only one to follow them so she could serve the ginger and cinnamon tea that was offered to visitors nonstop once the body had been taken away. Patience only stayed twenty minutes. No sooner had she left than, thanks to Manita, the entire Cité of Divine Power was aware that Yvrose had been given a large sum of money. For once, some good came out of a death in the Cité. Livio certainly wouldn't argue with that. He was stamping around in front of the house in his old clothes, swearing and shouting:

"Damn! Fénelon's gone back to Guinea! May the land of our ancestors welcome him!"

Around and around he spun, repeating the same phrase. People who died finally completed the voyage that had brought slaves from the coasts of Africa. Or so he believed, like lots of folks in this country. It gave him joy. And that was nice to see.

Several trucks had been hijacked. Rice, sugar, timber, gas, all the shipments trying to get south were confiscated and sold at cut price or divvied up in the Cité and roundabouts. There was talk of an imminent police operation against Joël and his men. Everything was quiet. Anyone who could move out did. Soline wasn't worried. Me neither. She told me that she'd seen and heard it all before, as long as she'd lived there, and was doing just fine, thanks be to God. "I'm a single woman," she'd added, "All I have is God and my neighbors, who are like family. Where would I go?"

I remember hearing Ma tell Andrise that Soline had had a male companion once, that they'd lived two years together, and that he'd left her for her good friend, "her accomplice," as Ma described her. They'd run side-by-side stands at the Hyppolite market. Soline almost lost her mind, Grand Ma said, adding that she wasn't sure if she'd ever really got it back. For eighteen years she'd held out hope that the man would snap out of it, return home, resume their normal life, marry her and have two kids, a boy first, then a girl, that was the order. "God is good," Ma would say to console her on the bad days when she would bitterly realize that she might not be able to have children anymore. She was fifty-six. The pastor's wife had advised her to try to make a life with one of the church widowers, one of the good Christians who had lost their partner in the last earthquake. Soline took it badly, insisting she already had someone in her life.

It was Easter. Kites filled the sky above the Cité, and from sun-up to sundown you could hear kids running, reading the direction of the wind, crying because someone had cut the string of their kite by attaching a blade to theirs. They ran shirtless, feet coated in mud, talking fast and sweating. Élise tried to shoo them from her terrace, but nothing worked. She was smoking more than usual, probably because she was afraid. Everybody was saying that Fanfan le Sauvage was preparing an attack against the Cité of Divine Power. Joël's gang was doing better business than his, the residents of Bethlehem were complaining, basic goods were cheaper in the Cité of Divine Power, all of which undermined his effectiveness and authority. Rumor also had it that the National Police was preparing an operation. Too many truck hijackings, too much extortion. Élise and her sister were wondering who would attack first, the police or Fanfan le Sauvage.

Yvrose was flourishing in her widowhood. She wasn't so skinny anymore. Andrise had attributed the weight gain to stress, without specifying if she meant more or less of it. Personally, I figured Yvrose had a lot less – even her head bobbled less – but who's going to admit aloud that their lifelong partner had been a constant source of stress?

A strapping fellow, just back from South Saint John, moved in with Old Nester. He called him Tonton. He seemed a little simple, was always wearing a pair of cut-off jeans, a yellowish polo that had seen better days, and a black cap with "L.A. Lakers" written on it in yellow. His name was Fatal, and he talked and laughed loudly, exposing decayed teeth. I'd see him go by every day carrying two five-gallon buckets of water in each hand. The old man had been alone since his wife and son died, and was still making little wooden keepsake boxes on which he carved "I Love You" or "Haïti." Now Fatal sold them.

Nestor always gave updates on his daughter, even when no one asked. All you had to do was say hello and he'd reply that Louisa was doing well, that now she had two daughters with American citizenship, which meant they'd never have to come live in the Cité of Divine Power surrounded by gang members and murderers like the ones who had killed Nestor's son. He never mentioned that his son, Daniel, had killed people too. It would have been too cruel to remind him of it. He just looked so old!

On the radio, the spokesperson for the National Police had been very specific, noting that there was a provision in the Penal Code for anyone who benefitted from theft carried out by gangsters, that they too would be considered complicit. By that measure, there wasn't one honest person in the Cité. Also guilty no doubt were the people who lived in the shanty towns above and below us dreaming of cheaper products. Carlos's face blanched when I told him.

"We absolutely have to get out of here."

I chose not to respond. It was ridiculous to always be having the same conversation, and always be forced to repeat the same "no."

Everything was calm in the Cité. People were afraid. We were all aware that everything and everyone was fragile.

Pastor Victor was a man possessed. By God. By the soul-saving mission He had conferred on him. To hear the pastor, the Lord had asked him during a face-to-face interview. People believed him. Grand Ma had no doubt about it. That's why she conscientiously paid her tithe, which incidentally was the only kind of tax she ever paid. Regardless of the heat, Pastor Victor always wore the vestment. It was what set him apart from the others. He and Andrise had five children who all looked like their mother. They never missed Sunday school, the Bible study group before Mass, which I'd never managed to join despite Grand Ma's urgings.

Victor's church was basic and blended nicely into the Cité. A large square room covered in corrugated iron, on the front of which was a wooden sign with MARANATHA CHURCH OF GOD written on it in red paint. Shiny beige floor tiles were the only luxury.

The first time I ever saw white people was at the church. Lots would come wearing T-shirts emblazoned with "Hearts for Haiti" or "Ohio loves Haiti." They always seemed happy in our sorry country.

We helped give a little meaning to their lives, and they brought us charity they'd collected on our behalf from their fellow countrymen. They offered us lots of prayers, all the while hoping that nothing would change for us so that there would be no shortage of good missions for years to come, which meant they would have more opportunities to save their own souls.

Victor was very proud of being able to bring foreigners to the Cité, and his wife clearly considered herself above everyone else, if only by the way she walked and talked and how fast she was to give advice on married life, virtue, and even eternal life. She wore a scarf around her neck that flapped when she walked and gave the impression she was being propelled forward. Any compliment on her elegance was met with an immediate "it's thanks to the grace of God" that came out in a whisper. Lots of women had tried to imitate her scarf, but the fabric they used must have been too heavy, or maybe they hadn't been able to obtain God's grace.

Their children had names pulled from the Bible: Jonas, Sarah, David, Esther, and Ruth. They were still young. Jonas, the eldest, was fifteen and preached in and around the Cité, the Bible under his arm, with conviction, eyes closed, arms open. He looked like an old man with his pointed shoes, gray pants cut from a heavy cloth, and white cotton shirt buttoned up to his throat. Victor pointed to his own children as examples of how other young people should behave. There was something not very charitable in that, which even Grand

Ma picked up on. She believed that I was also a model of goodness, wisdom, and selflessness.

Victor was one of the loudest residents of the Cité. He didn't look like it with his graying hair, his voice that went soft as soon as he left the pulpit, the gentle way he called everyone "my sister" and "my brother." The church was equipped with powerful loudspeakers which enabled Victor to break any and every silence during mass. There was a rumor that Victor had a soft spot for Fany. He was touched by her sadness, her solitude, her beauty, and probably also by the so-called "love sickness" people said she had. Whenever he ran into her, the man of God would stammer. He never managed to say a single thing to her, but his shyness got tongues wagging. The rumors made their way to Andrise, whose adopted strategy was to befriend Fany so she could better spy on her husband. She started by giving her a pink scarf with blue flowers (the kind light enough to flutter in the breeze), which Fany was delighted to receive. She invited her to join the Ladies of Maranatha group. They spent their time studying the Bible and going to prayer meetings in each other's homes and the homes of any churchgoer who invited them.

At first, the young woman, who only rarely went to church, was flattered, until she gathered, thanks to Élise who had ears everywhere, what Andrise's true motives were. She asked her sister to help her get the pastor's wife off her back. One Tuesday afternoon, seeing that Fany wasn't at Bible study, Andrise went to her house looking for her. She was afraid to let the girl out of her sight. She found Élise on the stoop, as drunk as back in her glory days, thanks to money she'd gotten from Fany to buy booze. Élise shooed away Andrise with her hand.

"I need to see Fany."

"She's busy. She can't see anyone."

"How's that? Who is she with?"

"That's none of your business, madame."

Andrise started shouting Fany's name, and tried to enter the house in spite of Élise who had pushed her back by menacingly blowing smoke in her face. I was out front, and stopped tormenting my phone to watch what was happening. It didn't look like Andrise had given up on seeing Fany, and Élise grabbed a broom leaning against the wall in the corner, and held it with both hands, her cigarette dangling from her mouth and eyes half-shut from the smoke. Fatal was passing by and set down his two buckets, adjusted his hat, and watched, making annoying chuckles. Andrise understood that she should leave before an audience gathered. She was crying, and her yellow scarf floated ahead of her in what was left of the daylight.

Fany never set another foot in church after that except on special occasions, funerals and weddings, and Victor still got flustered when she was around. Andrise had changed a lot, always anxiously looking around as though she was afraid the devil himself might appear. Victor was still sweet, though, with that welcoming and caring tone that put him squarely in the category of "good men."

Fatal had told a few people what happened, and they asked me if he was telling the truth. I told them I didn't see anything, didn't hear anything. I already had enough problems with Joël and Patience, who were keeping track of everything I posted on Facebook.

"*Dèyè mòn gen mòn.* Behind every mountain, another one is hiding," Grand Ma used to say. I was starting to understand. Joël knew people in power who had his back and he had theirs. He stirred shit up on command. He could have anything he wanted. VIPs sent their lackeys to him with envelopes, and he called people in high places on their cell phones. I wasn't wrong about Patience being a First Lady. Rumor had it that his gang members were unhappy, that the profits weren't being divvied up fairly. They were fine sharing food and other stuff taken off the trucks with the residents of the Cité, fine paying for funerals sometimes, but they also wanted a reasonable percentage of the cash being brought in for their work as soldiers.

Victor was holding forth at church, Soline was sweeping her porch, Élise had her headphones connected to her radio-telephone and was dancing with an imaginary partner, and I was waiting for Carlos. It was near six when I heard shots ring out. We were used to gunfire in the Cité. A few minutes later four armed men ran by, heading toward headquarters. A chill descended. Something was going on. Soline went inside and shut her door. Élise forgot her imaginary dance partner, removed her headphones, and went inside. I did the same. Tonton Frédo arrived shortly after. He must have run as fast as his alcoholic legs could go because he was out of breath. He had barely closed the door when the gunfire intensified and continued until dawn. Clearly, something was being celebrated. I thought about Grand Ma that night. She would have died from fear a second time. At around eleven I got up to see if my uncle was okay. He was asleep.

The sun had to come up eventually, the revelers would finally go to bed. But I didn't sleep much. I was afraid that a projectile would come through the rusty sheet metal. It wouldn't be the first time it happened in the Cité.

At seven in the morning, they announced Joël's death on the radio. He'd been killed by one of his own men, who was automatically declared "boss." It was ten o'clock once I was finally able to charge my phone at Andrise's place – when I saw photos on Facebook of what remained of Joël's body. His face was so bloody and swollen that it could have been anyone. His neck was destroyed, presumably from the bullets. His white undershirt was red, and both his arms were missing. The lower half of his body had been burned. Beer cans and bottles surrounded the corpse. His killers had partied all night. I started erasing everything that I'd posted about him so I wouldn't have any issues with the new boss of the Cité.

It was Livio who told me his name. They called him Cannibal 2.0. He'd eaten a bite of Joël's flame-broiled penis, which had earned him the sincere admiration of the gang members watching. It didn't take long for the video to circulate. I recognized him as the muscular tattooed guy. His eyes were glazed over and he was holding a machine gun in his right hand as he brought a piece of blackened meat to his mouth. I was so disgusted I threw up.

I thought about Patience. Had she been killed too? I didn't dare ask. I could have sent her a private message on Facebook, but was that wise? Maybe she'd been forced to give up her password? I didn't want to call Pierrot, unsure if he was in favor with the new boss. I looked through all the photos online for his face but didn't see him. Maybe he was the photographer? I did pick out Jules César, however. He seemed deep in concentration, a Galil in one hand and a beer in the other.

The new boss looked like he was part-Asian, his eyes mainly, and he was already starting to go bald. In the photo, he was wearing a shirt that was too tight, jeans and black velvet boots. A flood of other photos and videos got posted soon enough. He'd filmed and photographed himself. He gave his opinion on everything. Traffic, the high cost of living, the slums. The news. He said he wanted women to join him in the fight for social justice. In a matter of hours, Cannibal 2.0 had accumulated hundreds of "friends" and followers, including me. He'd made a spectacular leap from obscurity into the limelight, and already, I imagined, some of his men wanted to take his place.

In truth there wasn't a single teenager in the Cité who didn't dream about becoming a gang leader. It was one of the few accessible ambitions. With it came money, and a form of celebrity guaranteed by social media, traditional media, and the cowardice of elected officials.

Cannibal 2.0 wasted no time making himself known in the Cité. He strolled around, surrounded by his armed men. Pierrot was alive. He was walking with the group which had added two women – Natacha, dewier than ever, sweating from every pore, maybe a side effect of the creams she used, and a young woman I didn't know, who was dressed like a man and moved like a man. They let their pictures be taken, obviously. That was how 2.0 operated.

According to Fatal, what was left of Joël's body had been buried in the headquarters' courtyard. A shallow grave. And it was Jules César and the dreadlocked gangster who did the burying, the day after he was murdered. Livio, however, maintained that he had been buried under the basketball court. Victor dared a sermon on the sixth commandment – "*Ou p ap touye moun.* Thou shalt not kill" – which made the entire congregation uncomfortable. He received an order that same day to mind his own business if he wanted to continue officiating in the Cité.

I kept imagining scenarios for what might have happened to Patience. No one seemed to remember her, not even the "valiant women" she had welcomed and gifted rice, or Yvrose to whom she had given money for her husband's funeral. Everyone had erased the incriminating memory.

You had to be in the good graces of the new boss, show him what problems needed solving, remind him that the Cité had been abandoned before him, that he was the embodiment of everyone's hopes. A single death doesn't change anything.

One week after Joël's death, a black and white banner on which was written "Adieu Joël" was hoisted over the path leading to headquarters. It was up for two hours before a delegation, dispatched by Cannibal 2.0, arrived to take it down. The men fired off an automatic rifle to send a message to whoever had taken the risk. Photos of the banner had been taken and circulated on Facebook, but nobody could do anything about that.

After that incident, the new boss decided to have the Cité patrolled twice a day, early in the morning, and late in the evening. Taxes owed by merchants rose by ten percent. The gourde had dropped a lot in value, which meant the boss and his men had a loss to make up somehow, especially since one of Cannibal 2.0's promises was to give a little more money to his goons.

In Bethlehem, the boss had changed too. Fanfan le Sauvage had disappeared, and Dread Bob had replaced him. It was a clean job. Fanfan vanished like a puff of smoke. No corpse. Those once close to him had laughed when a journalist called them on the phone to find out what had become of him and they told him: "*Li ale Chili.* He went to Chile," a common expression ever since Haitians started emigrating there en masse.

Carlos was upset, the renovations for his house in Tabarre were taking longer than planned, mainly because of the high cost of building materials. Plus he wasn't selling as much booze, people had less and less money, and wholesalers were leaving the country, also en masse. The government needed to put an end to the reign of gangs, but instead, Carlos railed, the stranglehold was just getting tighter. His mother, with whom he lived, didn't want to move either. She had told him that it would be hard to live so far away, to leave her street, her church, her friends, that for an old person, a house was more than four walls keeping out the sun and the rain, it was a whole gamut of things that became like walking canes she could lean on, and if she didn't have them she'd fall and not get back up. Plus, here it's my home. Over there, it will be your home, with a wife: "*Granmoun pa rete kay granmoun.* One adult cannot live with another adult."

I'd looked at Carlos. So he had told his mother that I would follow him to Tabarre, even though I'd always said no. He lowered his eyes when he saw the stunned look I was giving him. I wanted to unleash a string of obscenities on him, to hit him. I didn't do anything. I needed him. He'd already cut back on his visits. Not more than three times a week. I had to be very careful how I budgeted. The phone was my biggest expense, internet expensive and unreliable, but it was the only way that I could be on social media. No point even looking at what the used clothing stands were selling anymore, or treating myself to a beer. The money I had was enough only to feed Frédo and me. Carlos had me by the stomach. He knew it. But the more I watched him, the more I knew that it would be impossible for me to spend every day at his side. I started to seriously consider what I'd do when he moved to the north of the capital.

I'd become skinnier than usual. Carlos asked me if I remembered to eat. It's good to be thin, he said, but you don't want to be a skeleton. Without realizing it, I had become withdrawn after Joël was murdered, and I spent too much time thinking about ways to make a little money. Carlos wanted me to ask him for the money, so I'd realize that I needed him, that I had everything to gain by going with him. I'd rather die. I'll never leave Tonton on his own. Grand Ma never abandoned me. I needed to see Pierrot. He was a moron but he might give me some suggestions, maybe even a little cash. I had a hard time thinking clearly. I saw no way out.

It was Pierrot who let me know about Patience, six weeks after Joël's murder. I'd sent him a WhatsApp message to ask him to come see me. He didn't respond but then he showed up, at the time I'd suggested. His right arm was still slung in a scarf, skinnier than the other one, and he held his gun with his left hand. He looked like he hadn't slept in several days. I sat down beside him on the stoop in front of the house. I noticed how some people were looking at us as they walked by. Disapproving, but also intrigued. Pierrot didn't even see them. He'd lost his soul a long time ago. Smothered by life. He'd seen lots of friends die, the same way he'd probably killed people whose only mistake was being in the wrong place at the wrong time, or having something worth stealing, or whose execution had been ordered by someone who didn't need to explain their motives.

I didn't know much about Pierrot. He was born in the Cité, and his mother raised him on her own. She worked as an in-home maid and got one day off a week, Tuesday. She'd get home around ten on those days. She worked far away, so it was better to wait until after the early morning traffic to get a seat on public transportation. Then on Wednesdays she'd leave before sunrise because she needed to arrive at her workplace by 7 A.M. She'd tried selling stuff, but that hadn't worked. She had two other children, younger than Pierrot, teenage girls who lived by themselves all week long. She'd have liked their big brother to look after them a little, but also thought that it was better that he kept his distance. The bad crowd he hung around wouldn't be good for the girls. On the occasions she responded to someone who asked about her son, she would sadly answer: "He's a lost cause." If he'd had a father, she thought, he wouldn't have turned out so bad. These past few months, with all these problems in the Cité, she would call Soline asking for news about her son, and then Soline would come out on her porch and bluntly ask me:

"Any news about your friend, Pierrot?"

Pierrot didn't have friends. He was looking out for himself, like all the other men walking around with guns not thinking of anything but the moment they were living. Like Grand Ma, Pierrot's mom might have dreamed that he'd become a doctor or an agronomist, to finally outmaneuver fate, and to be able to afford a nice house like the ones she broke her back cleaning six days a week for a wage so pitiful it wasn't enough to properly feed her daughters.

It was obvious that Pierrot was happy for the break, far from the other gang members, from the pressure from the Boss, which must have been considerable. That's how it was every time there was a new one. He didn't say anything. Waiting for me to start no doubt. I was the one who'd asked him to come, after all.

"How's Patience doing?"

My question actually made him jump. I couldn't help myself. I'd been thinking a lot about what had become of her since Joël's death.

"She's alive. That's all I know. The Boss doesn't want her going out. She knows too much. She had a few breakdowns after Joël, uh, left. But she's doing better. The Boss wants her to keep running the programs she started, the meetings with the women, the community restaurant that'll get kids at least one solid meal a day. She doesn't feel well enough to decide yet. She's resting."

"What do you mean, he doesn't want her going out? She's an adult…"

"Cécé, tell me you didn't have me come here to talk about Patience? In any case I'm not allowed to talk about the Boss's business. If you have nothing else to say to me, I'm leaving."

"No, that's not why I messaged you. I wanted to tell you that I'm looking for a job. I need money."

Pierrot appeared to be thinking hard, brow wrinkled, eyes half-shut. He suddenly got up, placed his gun on the ground, and dug into his pocket for a wad of gourdes from which he took three thousand-dollar bills that he handed me.

"I'll come back to check on you."

Then he headed in the direction of headquarters, looking more tired than when he arrived. He'd just made a large mental effort and had found nothing to say to me about my need for a job. Élise was across the way, watching us. As soon as Pierrot left, she started beckoning me over, making little "pstt" sounds. I ignored her. I was definitely not going to be the one who paid for her booze today. I left to buy myself something to eat.

I hadn't seen Félicienne since Grand Ma died. She was in front of her house where she had set up a large stand with bottles of cooking oil, packets of spaghetti, and boxes of cereal that she was selling. The house was squeezed between a pawn shop and a repair shop that fixed old television sets, radios and other electronic devices. They each played different music, at full volume. Over time, subjected to those high decibels, Félicienne had developed the habit of speaking very loud. Usually, I pretended not to see her. Féfé always had a dream to tell you about. You'd swear sleeping was her full-time occupation. According to her, dreams enable us to understand reality, to foresee what might happen. She would advise people to tell their bad dreams in the latrines to ward off bad luck. A loud "Cécé" forced me to turn in her direction. I walked toward her. She was giving me a big reassuring smile, her hands on her hips.

Félicienne had to be close to seventy. She looked in great shape, with her hair completely white and glasses whose dark blue frame made her seem even more cheerful. The first thing she had to tell me was that she had been to New York again to see her son Baptiste. He had had a second daughter with his wife. I almost responded that I hadn't even heard about the first one, but I didn't want to squash her enthusiasm, plus she did seem genuinely happy to see me. Féfé, as everyone called her, liked to touch whoever she was talking to. She adjusted my top for no reason at all, rearranged my hair which was pulled back with a scrunchie, stroked my face, smoothed my eyebrows, and wanted to know how I'd been doing since the death of my grandmother. She also asked after my uncle, whom she'd known since he was a kid. He and Baptiste used to play together sometimes, she reminded me. Then told me that Baptiste and his family were moving to Connecticut, where his wife had found a better job. She liked New York a lot, but she'd been told Connecticut was nice too. Different but nice. This way, she would get to know two places in that magnificent country.

Félicienne had had two kids. Two boys. The oldest one had emigrated fairly young to the U.S., taking advantage of a training program offered to some mid-level employees at the Ministry for Planning. He had decided not to come back. He married a woman of Haitian origin and made his life there, doing pretty well, and taking care of his mother as best he could. The second son worked as a door-to-door pharmaceutical salesman, was married, and lived in Port-au-Prince. He'd had a child out of wedlock that he gave to Féfé to raise. A little boy who was seven now, and went to school, like I did back in the day, with Maître Jean-Claude. Féfé lived in a two-room house with her grandson, her third husband, a man who never opened his mouth, his daughter, and his daughter's teenage son. I saw the little one a lot. When he wasn't at school, he was always sitting out front next to his grandmother, whom he called mom. I barely knew the others.

A devout Catholic, Félicienne never took off her rosary ring, saying she was praying for her sons, the country, and the pope. Between all the *you poor thing*s and the updates about her son Baptiste, my pride had taken a beating. Before letting me leave, she gave me a box of cereal and two little cans of concentrated milk.

I couldn't help thinking about the generosity that resisted the incredible violence, poverty and indifference that existed in the Cité. Féfé was one of the people who helped others, with the few resources at her disposal, which is what kept the fragile scaffolding of our community standing, despite the frustration and despair accumulating on it day by day.

Féfé's New York had been Grand Ma's dream, and that of everyone in the Cité and beyond. Often times it was just a generic word that symbolized an "elsewhere." The elsewhere where Tonton had left behind his soul and energy.

It was easy to get bogged down in the Cité. Literally. It rained last night, which meant piles of garbage here and there, puddles, and exhumed blue, pink, and white plastic bags. Faded umbrellas and tents made of stakes and thick plastic tarps, gray or blue, helped protect vendors from the sun. The city was one big secondhand market: clothing, electronics, kitchen appliances, furniture well past the point of utility. These things clogged the sidewalks and when finally someone good with their hands concluded that nothing more could be done with them, they ended up in the ravines, adding to the piles of junk. Sometimes artists would collect car parts and other discarded objects and transform them into works of art, coaxing beauty back into the garbage and scrap metal. People had stopped noticing the general state of deterioration, the chaos taking up every square inch of the Cité. Deep down, they were just as decayed as their surroundings.

I knew all the hallmarks of that exhaustion: the feeling that life can end at any second; the body that rebels and refuses to keep going, that caves to warning shots of hunger, of every kind of lacking; the mind withering, the onslaught of questions, the unresolved rage, the answers that never come.

It was hot. I felt like I was going to liquify, along with everything around me, the people, the worthless goods, the objects with no future, just like us. I felt like the rain would carry us to the ocean for a big bath of renewal and redemption.

Cécé la Flamme needed to make a comeback. She needed to reemerge from the fear that had kept her quiet since Joël's body was burned to a crisp and Patience disappeared. I'd taken those things as a chance for people to forget me. I thought I'd get my freedom back by no longer speaking. Instead, I realized I was just as dead, just as destitute, and just as abandoned as everyone else.

I ran into her but did not recognize her at first. She didn't have that scent anymore, that calculated slowness about her, the way she used to push back her braids. She was walking quickly, trying to leave the past behind her. And overcome her grief, perhaps. Patience had lost a lot of weight. Almost as if she had been trimmed down, front and back. Wherever the First Lady went, her fall from grace followed. Nobody who recognized her dared to look at her. And anyone who had at one time or another been hurt by Joël smirked as she passed and whispered that this was just the start of her comeuppance.

Patience was wearing a flowery shirt and jeans that were too big for her, and she must have been hot under her heavy braids. The light cotton shirt was soaked in sweat, especially under her armpits. She was now the gang's courier. Cannibal 2.0 struggled to hide his feelings for her. Patience had been kind to the men in the gang during her reign, even standing up to the boss on their behalf. Now Cannibal 2.0 wanted her to be his, and promised her even more power than she had had before. She'd asked for some time to think it over, telling him she needed to consult the loas and spirits who dictated her life, and might become violent if she disobeyed them.

Patience had looked at me. For several seconds. A cold, mean look that stopped me in my tracks. Why had I thought I could approach her, and talk to her? She'd never needed or deserved anyone's compassion. Cannibal 2.0 would never accept it if he thought people knew she missed Joël. She had no interest in sharing that past, or in playing the game of wearing your grief on your sleeve. Best leave that to the dead, of which, between here and Bethlehem, including Blessed Spring and all the other slums, there were more than plenty.

The dreadlocked guy, a well-known gang member, wasn't too far behind her but I hadn't noticed him. His job was obviously to follow Patience, discreetly. Hard to imagine a guy with that much hair being discreet, but I certainly didn't notice him until Patience was a ways off in her too-big pants and rubber-soled flat shoes that were likely easier to walk in than the pretty sequined sandals she wore before. In her left hand she was carrying an opaque black plastic bag, the kind people use to hide sad little items purchased at the market or the greasy bowl containing a meal just bought from one of the corner vendors or from Grand Ma, when she was alive.

Until then I'd had no idea how quickly grace can vanish from a person, or that you can voluntarily give up on seduction, turn off all the lights and shut all the windows of your life, waiting for an unlikely tomorrow.

The body had been decapitated. It lay in the alley between Edner's and Joe's. Yet no one seemed to be missing. The man's wrists were tied behind his back, and blood had turned his red shirt brown. It had dripped down to the belt of his light jeans, and wide red stains were splattered across his boots – walking shoes with soles edged in bright yellow. He was otherwise clean. The missing head must have been young. Robust. The shoulders were broad and the body muscular. A trickle of blood emerged from what was left of the neck, a sorrowful body grieving its head.

Joe and Edner had sent their little ones inside, though the children had no intention of obeying. Joe's eldest, a nine-year-old, had found the corpse when he went outside to piss in front of the house, his toothbrush in his mouth. The others were whining and complaining, they wanted to see. The most insistent one had already taken a beating intended to shut him up and dissuade the rest. They tried to peek through tiny holes in the rusty sheet of corrugated iron that served as the wall of Joe's house. On Edner's stoop, his wife, who gave birth pretty much every nine months, had a well-rounded belly, a baby in her arms, and a toddler clutching her skirt to stay upright.

I'd taken out my cell phone and started taking photos of the body and everyone standing around it. That's what set my Facebook photos apart: I didn't just show the corpse, but also how destitute people were, and their shock, their resignation.

Edner's wife spat. A thick, whitish gob containing all her anger and powerlessness. She roughly pushed aside the little boy hanging on her dress, which was really just a piece of cloth knotted above her breasts. The baby, a little more than a year old, fell onto its naked butt and screamed, and its mother screamed too, mouth full of saliva – must be a side effect of pregnancy. It took me a while to realize she was screaming at me, I assumed for stealing the spotlight from the headless body.

"Stop taking our photos, girl! You trying to show everyone how poor we are? Trying to make money off our images?"

I stopped right away. It wasn't the first time I'd been asked to stop taking photos, but it was the first time I'd encountered such hatred. People looked at me disapprovingly. I put my cell phone in the back pocket of my jeans and left feeling bad.

As soon as I got home, I posted the pictures on Facebook. Personally, I was moved when I saw what I'd captured. The baby in rags, sitting on the ground screaming, its too-skinny mother kept on her feet by anger alone, the infant in her arms, another in her belly like a threat, the shacks, the curious neighbors surrounding the dead man, the various colors of their clothing. All I wrote was, "*Nou tout pral pèdi tèt nou nan peyi sa a.* We're all going to lose our heads in this country." I got a flood of friend requests, some from well-known journalists, political figures, intellectuals.

A group of foreigners accompanied by a Haitian interpreter came to see me. They wanted me to talk, to give an interview, but all I could give them were yeses and nos. They wanted information I didn't have, to hear things I couldn't reveal or capture with words. Really, what more did I know than any other inhabitant of the Cité of Divine Power, of Bethlehem, of the capital, of the country, or of the world?

And then it was weird to find myself in the alley with a white woman and two white men in their sandals and shorts and this local man who translated everything I said. They looked out of place. They sensed it. They weren't supposed to be here either, they told me. The instructions from their embassy had been clear. So they suggested that we go somewhere else, where we could sit and have a bite to eat. That was fine by me. I was eager to eat, not because I was hungry but because I was afraid of going hungry, because of all past and future hunger. We walked to their car, which was parked at the entrance to the Cité, and got in.

The translator was also the driver. I sat in the back between the two men. When I was little, Mimose had told me that white people were werewolves who ate children, that they put them on their backs and flew away with them to cold and distant countries, where they were forever separated from their families. I looked at the man sitting on my right, and he smiled. These people didn't look like they wanted to eat me. They were chatting cheerfully in English. I didn't understand a word. The car headed toward the upper part of the city. Soon we passed the medical school, the Champ de Mars, Turgeau, Canapé-Vert Road. I knew we were in Pétion-Ville, but I wouldn't have been able to get around in this suburb where pretty much all the businesses from the lower part of the city had gone to set up shop, at first for security reasons and again when the 2010 earthquake ravaged the historic center of Port-au-Prince.

We were in Boyer Square, the guide informed me with a smile. As soon as he parked, four teenagers came over and offered to guard the car and wipe it down, then asked for money from the whites, who smiled stupidly. They followed us all the way to the entrance to the restaurant, but the expression on the security guard's face ended it there.

It was the first time in my life that I'd ever been in that kind of place. The only restaurant I knew was Morel's, which properly speaking wasn't even a restaurant. It was barely a step above what Grand Ma had been able to do, with its canopy over some plastic chairs that sagged with the customers' weight.

A young man in black pants and a white button-up welcomed us and asked if we wanted to sit outside or in the air-conditioned restaurant. The man who'd been sitting on my left and who the others called Matt wanted to stay outside. It was all the same to me. I was thrilled just to be there. Everyone in the group went to wash their hands, and they recommended I do the same. It was a far cry from the Cité. There was running water, and a toilet like you see in the movies. I started thinking about Grand Ma. In her whole life, I'm sure she'd never seen anything like what was in that restaurant.

I took a long time, or so I gathered from the look the guide gave me afterward. They'd been waiting for me to make up my mind. I went for something I knew: the *poulet pays*. It would probably be the same as anywhere else. I didn't like surprises.

The woman, Susan, grabbed a folder from her backpack, from which she took a few printed pages. Drew, the man on my right, asked the guide, whose name was Paul, to translate for me. The foreigners were asking me to sell them the right to use the photos I'd taken of the decapitated corpse and the people around it. Susan, smiling idiotically, spread two papers in front of me, for me to sign at the bottom.

"How much are they giving me?" I asked Paul.

"One hundred dollars."

"I want two hundred," I said, starting to eat before everyone else. They looked at each other, taken aback. I was playing big.

In general, whenever I posted photos, anyone could use them, and it had never interested me to know what they did with them. If these people didn't accept my counteroffer, I'd take the hundred dollars, which was a lot of money to me.

I was the only one eating, and I ate fast. I wondered how I could bring some leftovers home to Uncle Frédo. Matt said something, which Paul translated: "They agree to the two hundred dollars."

I wiped my hands with a paper napkin, pushed aside my plate, and signed with the blue pen Susan handed me, under the English text I didn't understand: Célia Jérome. I hadn't written my own name in a long time. It felt weird.

Matt settled the bill with a credit card. Drew withdrew a wad of hundred-dollar bills from his bag and gave me twenty of them, explaining that he wanted to use ten of my photos. I couldn't have cared less. I squeezed the bills into the wallet I had on me. Never in my life had I held so much money.

The car dropped me off on Harry Truman Boulevard and from there I had to walk home. I felt strange. I was afraid of the one-hundred-dollar bills getting stolen. People must have been able to tell that I was acting weird. Money... You get some, and it brings joy and anxiety all at the same time.

Someone had used a red spray can to paint "Vive Jésus" on the front of every house. Probably one of the many God-fanatics living in the Cité. Some of them would get up every morning at 5 A.M. and walk around with a megaphone shouting that everyone should accept Jesus. It didn't even occur to me to erase the graffiti. It would have meant scraping the wall already damaged by weather, and then the artist probably would have done it again. Carlos was bothered by it though, and took it as another opportunity to tell me that I had to leave this cité of lunatics and criminals.

He hadn't come all week, and expected to find me half dead from starvation. I was fine. I even had new gray leather sneakers, second hand, that I'd found at one of the stalls at the end of Rue Pavée. I'd put the dollars I'd made to good use. Seeing that I wasn't going to invite him in, Carlos asked me to go eat with him at Morel's. We didn't exchange a single word on the way. I didn't want to give him a chance to start into one of his usual lectures. In fact, I was planning on telling him that evening that I didn't want to see him anymore. I'd been offended when he told me how lucky I was that he'd invited me to live in his new house when there were lots of women who would love to be in my shoes, and meanwhile all I could think of was ending up like Yvrose. Carlos couldn't save me from a damn thing. I understood that elsewhere, in other neighborhoods, in other towns, life must look like something else, it must be closer to what a young person like me could dream up, but didn't you take the risk of losing yourself if you followed someone you weren't sure you could love? I was thinking a lot about Tonton, who had no one but me, while Carlos went on about the store we would work in together, the money we would bring in, the children we would have. I'd never thought about having children. Why bother having kids in hell? I felt a calm come over me as we walked, my decision was made. I would no longer allow this kind of conversation between him and me.

The fried food smelled good, though Morel wouldn't even look me in the eye. He had me down as in with the gang members with whom I'd spent an evening in his restaurant. Not that he would dare mention it to Carlos. I ordered a beer, pork, and fried plantains, Carlos got goat with rice and a Coca-Cola. It was his way of telling me that consuming alcohol was bad. The music was loud. He asked Morel to turn it down. He tried to take my hand. I pulled it away, with a briskness that took him aback. I looked around to see if anyone had noticed how ridiculous we looked. The only person in my life who had ever held my hand was Grand Ma, and that's how it should stay.

He was sweating. He looked like he didn't feel very well. I started drinking my beer. He looked at the plastic bottle of Coca-Cola on the table.

"I'm moving in two days. The boxes for the shop start leaving tomorrow."

"That's great."

"I'd like to be able to keep seeing you. I'll give you some time to decide whether you'll come live with me."

"I won't and this is the last time we'll talk about it. It just won't work. I'm not the kind of girl you need. I won't do housework and I won't cook. I won't sell in your shop, and I won't live in Tabarre, and I won't leave Uncle Frédo."

"You're going to starve to death here."

"We'll see. I wouldn't be the first. Thanks for your concern."

Our food arrived. I started to eat. He didn't. He seemed paralyzed. Someone had turned up the radio again. It was intended to attract customers. What I was eating was greasy and good. Carlos looked at me, subdued.

"I'm thirty-seven," he said.

I didn't see the utility in knowing his age. I looked at him without saying anything. He couldn't be the only thirty-seven-year-old man in the Cité of Divine Power and its surroundings.

"I want to start a family. Haven't we had a good thing going these past few months?"

"You got it all wrong, Carlos. You and I don't see what's been going on between us the same way. I'm not looking for a husband. I'm sorry that there was... a misunderstanding."

He put down the plastic fork with which he was eating his rice. His plate was nearly full. He tried to catch Morel's eye. Morel came to the table. Carlos asked him how much he owed. "Three hundred and fifty gourdes," said the restaurant owner, still not looking at me. He pocketed his money and left with my empty plate.

Carlos got up. He tried to hoist up his pants, but they hung hopelessly below his stomach.

"Should we go back to your place?"

"No. I don't feel like it. Actually, I'm going to stay here a while longer."

"What could you possibly do here on your own?"

"Charge my phone battery."

He looked really angry. I settled more comfortably into the chair, and added my comment to the others, all very violent, on a message posted by the President of the Senate. I didn't watch Carlos leave. I did feel a little sadness, though, when I finally looked up. I was relieved that he was getting away, far from me, from the city, to his brandnew house in Tabarre, but I had a dry throat and my stomach was in knots. Carlos wasn't a bad guy, apart from the fact that he could only imagine me behind a counter in his shop selling cases of Coca-Cola or preparing food, and all of it far from Uncle Frédo. Plus, he hadn't understood that, as far as I was concerned, it had never been a question of love or affection.

Suddenly, I felt something I had never experienced before. Like I was all alone. I could call Carlos, but I would regret it. His invitation didn't interest me. Jules César had just entered under the canopy. Morel looked panicked. Jules César saw me and came over to my table.

"How's it going, petite?"

He sat down across from me. It was the worst thing that could have happened. This blathering gangster was going to start going on about his mother or the people he had killed. He smelled of gasoline, as though he had been sprayed with it. It was really unpleasant. In one gulp, he downed half the beer that had been brought to him. It was too much for me. I got up abruptly, said goodbye, and left before he had a chance to say a word.

The news was all over the internet. A tanker carrying gasoline had been seized by Cannibal 2.0's gang. That explained the smell.

Pierrot was dead. It didn't take long for the news to spread through the Cité. People gathered near the entrance, not far from the arch, to see the body, photograph it, and comment on the death of such a young man.

"He was a gang member. How else could it end?"

"It serves him right. He killed people too."

"His poor mother will never get over it.'

"Well, if she'd dedicated her life to the Lord, if she'd said her prayers, it might not have come to this."

I heard these voices and words through a fog. I'd taken out my cell phone like the others and captured the image of the still body. He had a big hole between his eyes, and his right arm, dead before he was, was lying on his chest. The street smelled foul. It wasn't the body. He hadn't been dead that long, had died sometime in the night or early this morning. No. They had cleared a channel with stagnating water. It was eight in the morning. I'd been woken by Fatal shouting, inviting everyone to come enjoy the show. Some of the market vendors wanted to move the body to the other side of the street so that it wouldn't mess with their business, but the vendors on the other side of the street were against it. The compromise that seemed to be emerging was that the body be taken to the basketball court, but some residents of the Cité disagreed. A journalist showed up, and asked if the deceased was an important member of the 2.0 gang, but people didn't know how much influence he'd had, surely not a lot, otherwise he'd still have his whole head, rather than that bullet-riddled mug.

Dodo the Drinker arrived, shoving his way through the crowd and pushing an old homemade wheelbarrow whose wooden planks were covered in soot. He smelled of booze and sweat. He somehow managed to drag the body up into the wheelbarrow and took off with it in the direction of the Cité. Some of the gawkers followed. That afternoon, Fatal told me that Dodo had come to take the body on Pierrot's mother's instructions, and dropped it off at her house so she could bury her son like a good Christian and ask God all-merciful to pardon his mistakes.

It was hard for me to look at the photo of Pierrot's body. Occasional lover. Customer. Friend. Stranger. Nobody. He was all those things to me all at the same time. He was a lost boy, and the gangs had been his only future, like so many kids who lived in the lower city and elsewhere in the country. His mother wanted a private burial. Honor and her standing as a good Christian forbade any elaborate show of grief, and she didn't want her hypocritical neighbors who had never hesitated from commenting on her son's criminal proclivities from attending. According to them, she was supposed to feel liberated, and thank God for calling home this wayward child. But she was just as devastated by his death as by his life. And it wasn't God who had taken him. The decision had been made by Cannibal 2.0 and his men, criminals and thieves and who knows what else, the ones who had corrupted her son.

Facebook took down the photos of dead bodies that I posted. I even received a warning. I searched my phone for a photo of him alive. It was from three weeks ago. He was sitting on the steps at my place, supporting his right wrist with his left hand. He'd never admitted that he had any pain in his badly-treated arm. He looked worried and a little sad. Who said gangsters don't have consciences? I went on Google and did a cut and paste of the song that Madame Sophonie used to sing with us in class on Friday mornings my first year in school, one of the few ones whose words I knew:

By the light of the moon,
My dear friend Pierrot,
Please lend me your quill
So I might write a word.
My candle is out,
I have no more light.
Open up your door
For the love of God.

The thirty-three thousand two hundred and seventy-nine subscribers to my Facebook page responded en masse. By the end of the day, lots of new people had liked my page. If only they had been able to like Pierrot while he was alive, I thought, but what I thought was irrational and didn't matter.

I hadn't imagined it. Someone had knocked on the door. If Grand Ma were here, she would have loudly asked who it was in a tone that made clear the visitor wasn't welcome. I got up and turned up the light of the kerosene lamp by raising the wick.

"It's Jules," I heard through the door. "Jules César."

What could he possibly want at this hour? I asked him to wait. I definitely couldn't let him into my bedroom. I slipped on my sandals and went outside to meet him on the porch.

He was leaning against the low wall facing the street. I stood next to him, also leaning against the wall. We stood side by side for almost ten minutes without a word. I sensed that he needed to see someone who had known Pierrot, who was the one who'd introduced us.

"Do you want to go to Morel's?" he finally asked.

"No."

"I'll go get us two beers then. I'm thirsty."

There was no shortage of cold drink vendors in the Cité. They recycled old freezers and attached padlocks to them, then sealed them in the ground with concrete. They used large chunks of ice to keep their products cold, and they were open 'til late. Three minutes later, Jules came back with two very cold and already-opened local beers, and handed me one.

He gulped half of his bottle, then placed it on the wall so he could hold his head in his two hands. He was clearly upset.

"*Le petit* is dead," he started by saying, as if I didn't know.

By coming to see me, he was doing what he felt was his duty, it was like visiting the family to console them, and apologize, but there was no way he could visit Pierrot's mother.

He finished the of rest his beer, took out his phone, and dialed a number.

"Hey, yo! Bring me four more beers, you can have my empty."

We said nothing while we waited for the new beers. A young boy of around ten got there five minutes later carrying a white plastic bag with four beers in it. Jules took the four bottles out of the bag, placed them on the ground, put the empty bottle in the bag, and gave it back to the boy. He used his teeth to open one of the bottles, a quick, confident snap that showed he was in the habit of doing it.

"Pierrot let Patience escape. He gave his life for her. The boss wanted her to stay. He wanted her to be with him. He was in love with her. He let her stay in the room she'd shared with Joël, he gave her money she didn't use, she barely ate, she lost so much weight you could hardly recognize her. She asked him to let her leave. He refused, thinking she'd end up giving in. But Madame Patience knows how to read and write, and how to get along with the high-ups. She was the one who would go to the offices to collect money, to talk with the VIPs, gently tell them that if they didn't pay up the roads would be blocked. Cannibal 2.0 made sure she was accompanied by dreadlocks so that she'd come back after every pick-up. Some days, me and the guys get the impression that Cannibal is jealous of a dead man, he wants to take over everything that belonged to Joël. He's having a harder time dealing with Patience resisting him. Last night, he told her that he would no longer tolerate her turning him down, that he'd come get her in her room, that everything would be just fine. She decided to risk her life escaping. Pierrot was on watch and he just opened the gate and said goodbye. When Cannibal 2.0 went looking for Patience, around midnight, Pierrot told him it was pointless, that he'd let her leave around ten. Cannibal started yelling, took out his gun, and put a bullet in the kid's head."

Jules's voice choked up and he took a gulp from his beer that ran down his chin and onto his shirt.

"The Boss is offering three thousand U.S. dollars to whoever can get Patience back for him. He's gone crazy. He sprays himself with her perfume. It's weird, but nobody dares say anything. Patience left everything behind, her dresses, her pretty sandals, her perfumes, everything. All she took was her purse, probably because it had her papers. The kid didn't deserve this. He did a good thing. He was a nice kid, a helpful kid."

Jules César was weeping next to me. It was strange to see a murderer cry. It was genuine, he really did miss Pierrot, maybe saw him as family, a friend. I thought that he'd done a good thing too. It was too bad we couldn't talk about it openly, and make it known that there was still a little humanity in these young people who've been left behind, who know their lives will inevitably be short. Patience had regained her freedom. She must be far away by now, with her doubts and her truths. The First Lady had given up power and crime to stay faithful to her lover.

It was starting to rain. Big drops hit the dusty ground and it smelled good. Jules César stopped crying, and wiped his nose on his sleeve, which was disgusting. He told me he had to go. I watched him leave, walking resolutely through the mud, in the rainfall. I left the empty bottles on the porch and went back inside with mine, which I had only half-drunk.

I grabbed my phone which I'd left on the bed. Patience had posted a Facebook homage to Pierrot, whom she called a "hero," and internet users were taking her down. I "liked" her post, so then they went after me too. I shut off my phone.

I showed the lives of women in the Cité on social media. Élise was my first subject. She'd played along. It was less depressing than counting the dead, even though I still did that. I'd offered her some *tranpé*, her drink of choice, and she kindly sat in front of my phone to talk about her life. I was surprised to learn she'd always wanted a child, and that she hoped her sister Fany would have some one day. Her video was a huge hit. Then it was Soline's turn. She was modest, and described how she ran her business, her uncertainty, her fear of watching the Cité burn down, the feeling that she was stuck here in this place where gangs made the law. People started coming up to her in the streets to say they recognized her and to ask her more questions. She got into it and wanted me to record another video. Which had made me laugh. I guess everyone wants to be famous, after all.

More than 110,000 people had subscribed to my Facebook page. I got a private message from a lady who wanted to meet me. At first I thought she wanted me to interview her too. She asked me to send her my phone number. When she called, I knew right away that she wasn't from the slums. She was well-spoken, switching from English to French to Creole to explain that she was a marketing director and wanted to bring me on as an influencer. It was the first time in my life I'd heard that word. I went to meet her at her office, in a shiny new building on Airport Road. She had promised to reimburse me for my transportation costs. She explained to me that it would be advantageous, given how many friends I had on the various networks, to post the same stuff to my Facebook and Instagram accounts. She was a really chic lady. She introduced herself as Catherine Paris and asked me to call her by her first name. "Since we'll be working together," she added. I put her at around twenty-five. She had long, smooth hair, and she smelled good, like Patience, but you could tell she'd never lived in tough neighborhoods, and that she had traveled. I felt pathetic next to her in my crappy sneakers, wearing jeans and a second hand T-shirt that read, "I love Las Vegas."

She opened her computer and seemed pleased to tell me that my last video had gotten 72,000 views, adding an impressed "congratulations" and a wink. An older woman brought in coffee and water and waited to serve me. It was the first time anyone had called me "madame." Usually I got "petite." She asked if I wanted sugar. Of course I wanted sugar. Catherine didn't take any. I was surprised to see her drink her coffee bitter. Must have been an elegance thing.

"I am truly so happy that you agreed to meet me, Célia. I promote various consumer products, and I'm looking for people like you, *des gens comme toi*, with a large following on social media, to help me. Your job will be simple. I'll give you samples of what I want you to show our target audience, people from your milieu." She blushed when she said *des gens comme toi*. "I'll explain what I want you to do, and I'll pay you every month. You can make a lot of money this way, you know."

The coffee was very good. I'd put a lot of sugar into it. The cups were pretty, if a little small. Catherine got up to grab a piece of paper from a binder, wearing very high heels. How could anyone walk on those things? She sat back down and opened a folder, then took out some photos: an energy drink in a plastic bottle, a skin-lightening cream, a deodorant supposed to protect you for forty-eight hours, a pomade meant to make your hair grow.

I could have held back but it came right out: "Vous utilisez ce savon vous-même, Catherine? Do you use that soap yourself?" She blushed down to her roots and brought the cup of bitter coffee to her mouth, leaving the imprint of her red lips on the rim. She shook her head no and smiled before going on. "No, I don't need to, but there is a huge market for these products, and this one is better for your skin. Women. . . are looking for the best, and that's what my associates and I offer."

I smiled because I could tell she'd been that close to saying "women from your milieu." Catherine Paris was very confident, and clearly she knew how to make money. She paused, then continued: "You've found yourself a real gold mine here, Célia, believe me. It's lucrative work, and you're going to be very comfortable financially. 'Cécé la Flamme' can be made into a business. You just need to take a picture of yourself drinking this drink or using one of these products. Don't worry about the lightening cream, you already have fairly light skin. You can just pretend you're using it. That should work."

She had looked at my clothes while she talked. I guessed that she felt a little embarrassed about her pitch for the lightening cream. The contrast between what she was wearing and what I was wearing was enough in itself to show the divides in this country.

"How much will I be paid?"

"I'm going to give you thirty thousand gourdes every month, and of course you'll get these products for free for your personal use, and if you want, you can sell them. I'll give you a discount on them, and that way you can make even more money."

"I want sixty thousand gourdes," I said, looking her straight in the eye. As a matter of principle, I always multiplied an offer by two.

"Fifty."

"No. Sixty. On top of the discounts you mentioned. Even though, for now, I don't want to sell anything. And before I start, I want another phone. Mine doesn't take great photos."

We both looked at her Samsung, the latest model, sitting on her desk. She seemed to think about it, looking at the photos spread in front of her, as though the answer would come from them.

"Fine. Sixty thousand gourdes and a phone that's better than the one you have. You start tomorrow."

"I want an advance."

Catherine let out a big laugh. I was very calm. I poured myself some more coffee and added lots of sugar.

"You are a tough negotiator, Célia."

"Thank you, Catherine."

A man walked into the office just then. His skin was as light as Catherine's. She started speaking to him in English. He extended his hand, which I shook. I assume Catherine was talking about me because he was looking at me and smiling. He left and I never figured out if he could speak Creole or French. Though what did I care.

"I'm going to have a check drawn up for you right away. You'll need to sign a short contract, to be sure everything's clear. I'm also going to get a box ready for you, with all the different products. That good?"

"Yes, but I'd prefer cash. And don't forget the transport money."

"That shouldn't be a problem," she replied with a smile.

I'd used some of the money I made from selling the decapitated body photos to pay for the mototaxi that had brought me here and was waiting outside. It was expensive. Airport Road was pretty far from my place. Catherine had me wait alone in her office, and I snuggled into my chair. It was turning out to be an excellent day.

Straddling the motorbike on the way home, with the little box between the driver and me, I felt good. I occasionally squeezed the envelope of 30,000 gourdes in my bra, which felt good too. I was supposed to return the following week to pick up my new phone.

I spent my time photographing myself drinking what was actually a repulsive beverage. To be honest, I cheated. I mixed it with water. In a comment on one of my tweets, someone informed me that abusing energy drinks could cause high blood pressure. Doesn't matter your age. I staged myself using the deodorant, whose smell I liked, and then the hair gel and the skin-whitening cream. A lot of my "friends" accused me of encouraging young girls to bleach their skin. They were right. That was exactly my new job. I didn't respond.

I bought a new shirt and new pants for Uncle Frédo at one of the secondhand stands. He was looking too much like a homeless person. He clapped his hands like a little kid. He must have felt handsome in the light-blue, long-sleeved shirt and gray trousers. And it did give him a different style. Seeing Tonton happy made me happy.

Soline looked kind of crazy that day. She had wrapped a white cloth around her head, probably a man's old undershirt, and stuck almond leaves in it. "I'm on edge," she explained. Some lady who sold the same spices as she did had set up a stall next to hers. They had almost come to blows. She'd decided to take two days off to let her nerves settle. She was drinking herbal tea too. I offered her some hair gel and deodorant. She was sleeping in the clothes of her man who had left her for another woman. I'd seen her early that morning with her compress, checkered pants she couldn't zip, her flowery nightgown over the pants, and a gray button-up over the nightgown. He'll never come back, I thought, if he runs into Soline dressed like that. Not that it mattered how my neighbor dressed, he wouldn't be coming back. The guy had to be pretty old by now.

When Soline was home, she would bring me and Tonton food. That's how it was in the Cité. Neighbors exchanged meals. Ma used to with Yvrose, Fany, Old Nestor, and Soline of course. I always gladly accepted Soline's food. Though I never cooked myself. So I was happy to be able to give her products I had come by for nothing.

I didn't want to be so distracted by my new job that I stopped paying attention to what was going on around me. Fatal had been badly beaten up the night before, but they let him live so everyone would understand they needed to keep their mouths shut. Fatal, apart from deploying his trap more than he should have, even gossiped about things he hadn't seen. People had heard him talking about Pierrot a few times, and also making fun of the boss who'd lost the woman he loved. He was left in front of Nestor's door, who dragged him inside and applied a compress to his swollen face. Nobody saw him for a whole week, until the need for water forced him out. After all, Nestor certainly wasn't going to go fetch any. They hadn't cut off Fatal's tongue, but they may as well have. He didn't acknowledge anyone, didn't even say hello back. He kept his eyes down so he didn't have to see the cruel and mocking looks he got, and hurried down the alleys, his cap tight on his head, body pulled forward by the full buckets he was carrying, heckled by little kids who reminded him that he'd taken a beating. Dodo and Lorette were no longer the only ones subjected to frustration-fueled jeers. People seemed to have forgotten that everyone and everything in the Cité of Divine Power was at the mercy of Cannibal 2.0's gang. Soline kept making huge sighs so loud you could hear them from far away, and they said a lot about a lot of things. She let one out, hiding behind her compress, when she saw the poor guy walking fast like he wanted to outrun the kicks he'd taken, and the rifle butts, get away from the death he'd come face to face with and which was chasing him all the same, along with the shame and the sorrow he felt.

I posted a photo of Soline on my Facebook page along with her rescue remedy for "shocks," intended for an entire country paralyzed by its weaknesses and a mutual loathing between the local and expat communities that has only grown, reinforced by years of capitulations and bad habits.

Cannibal 2.0 had his own official accounts on Twitter, Facebook, and Instagram, and maybe more. He'd sent me a friend request that I ignored. I knew that I would have to accept it. He didn't rely on the same methods as Joël. He hadn't summoned me. I could recognize the ones who worked for him, from their comments. They wrote on my wall that Cannibal 2.0 was the only one who cared about the poor, they thanked me for showing how people had been left to their own devices, and urged me to talk about the Boss's accomplishments, even though his most notorious acts since taking charge were Pierrot's murder and poor Fatal's beating. He spent his time comparing himself to Joël and looking for Patience. He'd posted photos of her, begging people to tell him where she was in exchange for a reward, but the photos he posted didn't look like her anymore. She no longer had that face or that soul. She had died with Joël and had chosen to make way for another woman, maybe the one she had been before she had met her gangster lover. No one would recognize her from those photos.

But words, photos, prayers couldn't do anything about the accelerating deterioration of life in the Cité of Divine Power and the slums around it. They embodied every urban failure, and the hard life. It didn't matter where in the country you were these days, you could feel life's rough edges. We were all trapped by a situation that had been too long ignored, people refusing to see, refusing to hear.

Victor railed against the devil, and his congregation responded with energetic *amens*. I posted pictures in which I, Cécé la Flamme, lathered myself with cream supposedly able to lighten my skin. And perhaps Pierrot's mother found some solace in telling herself her son was in heaven. It was too bad that lies did nothing to serve peace.

The news spread quickly. The police were waging an operation against Dread Bob and his soldiers in Bethlehem. The gunfire could be heard in the Cité of Divine Power. Then a flood of rumors. Plus news, photos, videos circulating on WhatsApp groups. The commentators made it clear by the tone of their voices that Dread Bob was the hero. Amid the shoot-out, he had called in to a radio station and promised hell to government officials and threatened to set the whole country on fire.

The situation was making the members of the Cannibal 2.0 gang nervous, and they started shooting their guns too, like a conversation where everyone wanted the last word. Élise let out a cheer at each burst that came from the Cité of Divine Power, no doubt to lift her sister's morale, since Soline was disgusted by all of Bethlehem and considered Dread Bob the heir of Fanfan le Sauvage. In her mind, all the criminals in Bethlehem needed to be eliminated to avenge Pipo. Meanwhile, she was praying, louder than usual though, which scared me. She kept shouting "Jesus" and sounded like she was crying. I didn't know what I could say to console her, and then I wondered if it was smart to go out at all.

Residents of the Cité went into lockdown for one day and one night. It must have been worse in Bethlehem. Though people were quick to forget. Until the next escalation. There were lots of comments about the exploits of Dread Bob who was now demanding he be referred to as "God's soldier," judging that he'd escaped death thanks to the Almighty, and insisting that residents of Bethlehem attend daily prayer meetings. He had personally executed two members of his gang whom he suspected of betrayal.

Cannibal 2.0 sent patrols through the Cité. Sweaty and heavily armed men in dark glasses paced up and down the alleys. They made it seem as if a police raid was imminent. It made me smile. I think the new boss was jealous of Dread Bob getting to talk on the radio. Even the chief of police had made a statement about him, inviting him to lay down his weapons and surrender. On TV and radio, entire shows were devoted to him. An article listing his crimes was pasted across the front page of the country's oldest newspaper. Cannibal 2.0, compared to Dread Bob, was an ordinary criminal, a small-time highway bandit. He was starting to think his men hadn't forgiven him for Pierrot's murder. I for one knew that Jules César still blamed him. He couldn't understand the Boss's obsession with Patience and all the time he invested in looking for her, incapable of moving on. He had promised that social programs would get going once "la madame" returned, but everyone knew she wouldn't be coming back. He sent the jittery bald guy and the tall skinny guy to distribute rice, sheet metal, wood, gas, and various other products they stole from passing trucks, but without checking whether people needed them or not. The merchandise was resold on the sidewalks.

Cannibal 2.0 had lost all his muscle. His clothing had become too big for him, and the tattoos on his neck and arms made him look like a sad little boy. If it weren't for his two armed guards, the nine millimeter pistol he packed at his waist, and the Uzi in his right hand, which forced you to take him seriously, he wouldn't have even been noticed.

Still, for someone who looked so ordinary, he moved a lot of money. Drugs were in high circulation, drawing junkies from other cités and small-time dealers who came to stock up. Cannibal 2.0 gave money to his men, and less pressure was being put on merchants. Residents now only had to pay up once a week to be left in peace.

The patrols continued but lacked conviction. I had removed the bits of plastic Grand Ma had used to stop up the holes in our ventilation blocks to prevent *movezè*, bad air, from entering the house. The plastic had been there for years. It had become brittle, light brown, opaque, though it did keep dust out of the house. But now I had a proper observation post. I could see people going by without them seeing me. And funnily enough, I was noticing details that I couldn't see up close. Élise losing her hair, the bald patch in the middle of her skull, something I thought happened only to men. Her sister Fany, since the incident with Andrise, only left the house twice a day. No more peaceful moments surrounded by her plants. You'd see her first thing in the morning hurrying to the latrine, a tiny cubicle that stank and caused no end of squabbling in the Cité because often enough you'd have to share it. She'd stay in there for almost a half-hour. And then when the sun started to set, she'd go out again to water the plants. She must have been of the same mind as Ma, who used to say plants need watering before sunrise or after sundown, although, in fairness, Ma never had any plants, apart from a cactus that didn't need much watering at all. I don't know what happened to it after she died. The pot it was in disappeared.

Jules César stared hard at the house when he passed by. He must have felt he was being watched. He was in boots, deliberately stepping in muddy rivulets on top of which floated puddles of waste motor oil, which was supposed to be a deterrent to mosquitoes breeding.

Were these soldiers baking in the heat even alive, with nothing to their names but the hour that had just gone by? The police wouldn't come. They all knew it. The policemen who lived in the Cité of course did too. There was nothing to report. A popular song was playing on a nearby radio. Everything was broken beyond hope.

I was happy to see Carlos again. He arrived without warning, knocking on my door at six thirty. Faithful to his habits. Even in how he dressed. It seemed like a long time ago that he'd moved away, but it had only been a month. He was smiling in a way that I took as his asking me to forget that we'd parted on bad terms. I still had nothing to say to him. He wanted to know how I was doing. Just fine. He noticed my new clothes, my new shoes, and the boxes in the middle of the room that held the products I was promoting. They were giving off a nice smell, which must have been the deodorant and the lotion. He didn't dare ask me to explain. I wouldn't have. We avoided any contentious subjects, which didn't leave us with much to say. I no longer needed his thousand gourdes. Plus, I didn't want there to be any confusion. All of a sudden it went dark. We could hear the buzzing of mosquitoes over our voices. The electricity had gone out. I lit the kerosene lamp. He asked about Uncle Frédo. I almost burst out laughing. I knew it was just to fill the silence. Still, I answered that he was doing well, and I asked him how business was going in Tabarre.

"Not as good as in the Cité," he snorted. "There are lots of stores around that are the same as mine and bigger. I'll need to diversify the business. I'm giving it some thought."

I was on the verge of suggesting he sell Catherine Paris's products. The idea made me laugh. He gave me an anxious look. I lied and told him I was sure he'd find a solution very soon.

"I miss the Cité of Divine Power," he told me. "Now I understand why my mother didn't want to move. Plus, I'm really lonely. I hired a kid to help me. No gang leader has come asking me for payment, at least not yet."

He was thinking. The lamp lit up his neck and part of his face. He had lost a little weight. Must have been the stress of the move, maybe also because his mother was no longer cooking his meals.

"I think I would like to leave. And try to build a life in a safer country, with more rules. I mean, it doesn't get much worse than here, in terms of human dignity. It's complicated to get an ID card, to have enough to eat, security, electricity…" he said, lifting his hand towards the ceiling, as if he needed proof the bulb wasn't turning on.

He wanted to add something, but his voice went hoarse. I looked at my shoes just in case he was crying. I didn't want to see it. I was sitting on the bed and my feet didn't touch the floor. The cot was high. Grand Ma had put some old clothes under the mattress to make it even higher.

"I love my country. And I'm sure there are things that could be done. But I'm tired. So tired," he said, stretching, making the chair creak.

"Are you hungry?"

"Yes," I replied.

Both of us got up. Our relationship had just advanced to the next stage. Our minds at ease. We expected nothing from each other.

Some people will never leave. It hasn't even crossed their mind. It's not that life here was beautiful. Or that they were unaware that death wasn't far behind. They simply didn't have the means to go anywhere else, beneath another piece of sky that would be different than this one. Bethlehem or Blessed Spring, same problems, same chances at happiness. There were also some people who could only assert their domination in a forgotten place like this, where souls wander sadly and desperately, seeking to be held and looked after. If only to create the illusion of living,

    I listened to the mad folk going by. To understand. To try to. Lorette would tell people she was a *grande dame*. I've known her forever, but she doesn't know anyone. That's how it is with *grandes dames*. It's on other people to remember them, never the other way around. Grand Ma used to give her something to eat on days when she kept her clothes on. Several layers that didn't hide her thinness, and which she would abruptly take off making obscene gestures that made the kids laugh and angered the adults. Ma advised me not to watch. But I'd often disobeyed my grandmother. I would know Lorette was nearby when I detected her pungent smell of urine, which was the first excuse people gave who threw stones at her to keep her away. Lorette frequently had injuries. On her head especially. I was astonished she was still alive. In some ways she symbolized this cité. This country. She was resistant to the hard knocks. The neglect. Her dirty, tangled hair and her twisted, worn-down shoes told life-stories far more touching than the ones Livio invented about her to make people laugh at vigils. Lorette could have been Mimose, Lana, Soline, Grand Ma, except she'd had even less luck, and had cracked under the various pressures. One day she'd land in the Cité of Divine Power and never left. Homeless and poor, she gathered everything she came across, living under pieces of plastic, surrounded by objects she'd picked up, everything from empty bottles to human bones. One morning they'll find her in an alleyway, dead, along with her past, her tragedies silent or untranslated.

I listened to the Cité. Lying in the heat. Tonton was asleep. The door to his little room was open. Any trick to get the air to circulate was welcome. But the air did what it wanted. I fanned myself and shooed away the flies with an old newspaper that left my fingertips black. The headline story talked about the umpteenth renewal of the United Nations' mission. The Security Council. Things that, when it came down to it, had nothing to do with us.

Old Nestor was banging his hammer so loudly he could have been under my bed, Fatal's radio was blaring a talk-show whose hosts were vying to be the most outrageous and also most idiotic. Another radio in the neighborhood was tuned to the same program, which made for a funny echo. Fatal and the other listener must have been competing – a matter of volume, the brand of receiver – a common occurrence in the Cité.

The noise outside had to have been making it even hotter and riling up the flies. It was impossible for me to sleep. Uncle Frédo was snoring softly. My phone showed 10:37 and three missed calls from Catherine Paris. I hadn't posted in four days. I was tired of the same photos, the same products, writing the same bullshit. During our last conversation she'd suggested that I show more shoulder, my bare feet. "And what next?!" I'd replied. She realized she'd better not push it with me. I'd read the one-and-a-half-page contract she'd had me sign carefully, and at no point was there any mention of nudity. She was quick to appease me, and our mutual silence revealed her embarrassment.

I would put on my headphones and return her calls after I ate. My stomach was empty. I had 273,000 subscribers, but she had 60,000 gourdes that I couldn't spit at. I was fine with showing my feet alongside the lightening cream as a show of good faith, but I had the remnants of a dark-blue polish on my nails that I couldn't even remember putting on. I needed to find some nail polish remover.

I lifted the mattress to grab money for food and the remover. I'd opened a bank account but hadn't yet found the motivation to go deposit any of the 60,000 gourdes I'd gotten for my third month of work.

My feet were sweating in my sneakers. I should have washed. Then I wouldn't be feeling my body prickling. Or maybe it was all in my head. I'd learned that women who whitened their skin with soaps like the one I was promoting felt a prickling sensation whenever they went out in the sun. But I've never actually used it.

The vendors were grouped according to what they sold. The ones who sold cosmetics had basins of every color that held nail polish, nail polish remover, creams and soaps that promised cleaner skin, by which they meant lighter. They discolored their own skin, too, you could tell from the black stains on their faces and their too-dark knuckles. The brand I was promoting on social media was in all the basins, though the competition was fierce. There were at least six brands. Despite myself, I felt a burst of pride at seeing Catherine's products everywhere, proof they were in demand. The soap cost fifty gourdes. Its glossy cardboard box was white with embossed gold lettering that read: BABY WHITE. I bought some nail polish remover and pink nail polish from a vendor who looked around the same age I was. She seized the opportunity to ask if I wanted to smell a bargain perfume, which she removed from its packaging, delicately removing the cellophane wrap protecting the box, something she probably did multiple times a day. And then she rewrapped the bottle just as dexterously when she saw my grimace after I sniffed it.

I bought a small jar of concentrated milk, some bread, corn mash, and sugar. When I got back, Uncle Frédo was sitting up in bed with his shirt off. As usual, we said nothing. We were intimate strangers. To get up in the morning, I needed to know he was alive. I wasn't sure what he made of me, but I felt a connection between us. There was Grand Ma, this house, and a story neither he nor I could tell. And since we couldn't, we went on expressing it with large spells of silence, and through smiles, and that suited us just fine.

We ate without a word, dunking chunks of bread and our fingers into the mash, sugared heavily the way we liked it, the way Grand Ma had taught us. Élise was in the middle of telling Livio he was a crook, that he'd yet to deliver the five buckets of water he'd already been paid for, everyone else adding to the noise: Victor and his many followers, Nestor, Fatal, street vendors, even Catherine who called just then, making my phone vibrate. Uncle Frédo didn't have a phone, he barely had a voice, and he didn't walk very fast, but he was part of the balance. At least of mine.

The pink nail polish went a little over the edges of the nails of my big toes. The final look wasn't great. But with the photo taken sideways and my legs crossed, you couldn't tell. It took me about ten takes. Grand Ma would have been amazed to see photos that sharp captured with a cell. The phone vibrated. It was Catherine. I had the feeling she always had her eyes on her phone or her computer. I'd only just posted the photo she'd suggested.

"Hello Célia! I just saw the photo, very pretty, very well done. The brand name is very clear on the tube of cream."

Only Catherine called me Célia. Hardly anyone knew it was my name. Natacha was one of the few, but it wasn't the sort of thing she thought about. She was pregnant again – probably by one of the Cannibal 2.0 gang members – and puffy, and dark blotches appeared on her damaged skin.

"Our sales have taken off. I love experimenting with new marketing strategies... So I'm thinking, Célia, that you should keep talking about things that happen in the Cité, that's how you'll pull in more *friends*, *subscribers*, and *followers*. You know, photos like the ones of the headless body, videos where women talk about their lives..."

I was disgusted. I hated her shrill voice, her certainty, her Anglicisms I didn't understand, her self-involvement and single-minded obsession with the need to see her profits grow. I told her I was having trouble hearing her, that I needed to hang up. It was totally plausible. Telephone communications were usually pretty terrible.

I had a few too many of her products in my bedroom. I would give them to Soline and she could do whatever she wanted with them. I had trouble imagining her whitening her skin, but it was up to her.

No need to knock, she was out front, cooking on her little porch. She was sitting in front of a small charcoal stove, trying to revive the embers with a piece of cardboard, and complaining that the charcoal was no good, definitely made from damp wood. A lid covered the pot so I couldn't see inside, but since there was no particular smell, it must have been plantains or some kind of tuber. I set down the cardboard box overflowing with creams, deodorants, soaps, and hair gel. Soline looked at me suspiciously. The woman was honesty incarnate. I almost burst out laughing. I did not regret coming over. She didn't treat me like a little girl anymore. Grand Ma had been dead two years now, and I was doing fine on my own. She could see that. She didn't ask me how, but believed that my grandmother had prayed enough, and instilled enough of a work ethic in me, for me to figure things out on my own.

"Neighbor Soline, I do marketing for these products on the internet." Her eyes opened wide as I spoke. "I have a lot of them and I thought I'd give you some. You can either sell them or give them away."

She handled the products in the box and squinted her eyes to try to read the information printed on the tube of skin-lightening cream. She gave up, deciding to smell it instead. She was going to need glasses.

"But this stuff is so expensive…"

Fifty gourdes represented a lot of money for Soline who, some days, would only make ten gourdes selling her garlic.

"I got it for nothing. Actually, it's for work, kind of. I pretend to use this stuff on social media, and I get paid."

"You pretend you're working?"

"No, well, not exactly. I post photos of myself with the products to show them to lots of people who see them and buy them."

She looked at me in disbelief. It was hard to explain how it worked to Soline. I ended up explaining that giving them to her was a kind of advertising. She looked relieved, and told me with a mischievous smile that she'd sell them starting tomorrow. She wanted me to stay and eat some sweet potato. I agreed and sat down on the low stool next to hers.

She served me a delicious potato on a chipped plate she'd fetched from inside the house. I used the fork she handed to me to break it into several pieces by applying light pressure with the tines. White steam came off the different bits. There wasn't any meat or sauce, but it was good.

Soline sat eating with her hands as the day came to a close. It was moving, in a way. What is it about the silence between two people that could muffle the noise of the Cité? At least that's how those special moments with Tonton, and now Soline, felt to me.

"My little sister, Mislène, loved sweet potatoes, just like you. It's been twenty-five years now since she died. She was a passenger on the boat *Neptune* that wrecked in 1993. It ran between Jérémie and Port-au-Prince."

She paused, chewing for a long time on a piece of potato. You had to go easy with sweet potato, otherwise you could get the hiccups. For me, there was no escaping it. I had already released a little harbinger squeak along with a shake of my shoulders. Soline went into the only room in the house, and returned with water in a green plastic cup. She told me to drink seven mouthfuls in a row. It was the best remedy for hiccups, she claimed.

"My sister always got hiccups too. No more and no less than seven swallows. She was so happy to be able to come live in Port-au-Prince. It was the first time she'd left her home province. She was supposed to join me. She'd brought along sacks of coconuts so she could start a business. Apparently, the cattle on the same boat, and the sacks of coconuts, served as buoys for some passengers who were able to make it to the coastline of the town of Miragoâne. More than two thousand people perished in that shipwreck. It was during a difficult time, or more difficult, I suppose, than others. The country was under an embargo following the coup to oust President Aristide. It was Ash Wednesday, after a strange Kanaval where the dancing and celebrating weren't enough to mask people's despair. I had a lump in my throat. It's crazy how, sometimes, we can sense that something bad is about to happen."

Night had fallen as Soline spoke. We were each holding an empty plate. A bulb had gone on in Yvrose's shop. Feebly lit. That's how it was in the Cité. The houses were tied into the city's grid thanks to clandestine connections. Those weak yellow filaments were a good indicator of how the widow was doing: she was tired and barely holding on without Fénelon. Now that the funeral was over, she was one of the few people who spoke of him as a good Christian. The little shop was on its last legs, and you could tell it wouldn't be long before it closed altogether. Yvrose was tired. She went to bed at night only to wake up the next day with more gray hair.

The night was all of a sudden put on pause. I reached out my hand to grab my phone and check the time, but the movement was too brusque, and it fell off the chair with a thud. I sat up in bed. A long burst of machine gun fire persuaded me to lie back down. I had to wait until my eyes got used to the darkness to find the phone. Tonton's bed creaked. I hadn't imagined it. What was going on outside was huge, as big a deal as on the night my grandmother died. So who would die in the Cité tonight? The shots had managed to wake my uncle up. He was making questioning grunts that made me smile. You'd think he'd be used to it.

I could make out the phone under the chair. I needed it to know what time it was. It was 11:35 P.M. I hadn't been sleeping long. It was hot, I'd sweated, and the neck of my top was uncomfortably damp. I had fallen asleep completely dressed, as I often did. The last thing I remembered was checking the WhatsApp status of people in my contacts. It was one way to pass the time.

The day and the afternoon had been calm, so what had happened? Now I could make out voices amid the shots. People were laughing as they ran noisily through the alleys. I tried to recognize the voices, but couldn't. It sounded like a big party. Whoever was out there was happy, they were drinking and breaking empty bottles against the walls. The laughter was raucous, satisfied. Were it not for the constant gunfire, you'd almost want to go outside and join the fun.

As the night went on the shots became less frequent. I fell back asleep around 5 A.M. to the voice of someone drunk and insulting at great length someone else whose mother was a whore, father was a dog, and himself a gay sex worker.

Elected government officials, to make people forget they weren't doing anything with their mandates, had taken it upon themselves to legislate against homosexuals, and now physical and verbal assaults on that minority were on the rise. It didn't matter that women were being battered, and children abused and uneducated, that the laws were antiquated or obsolete, the public university in ruins, the prisons overflowing, the courts overwhelmed. What mattered was to not be homosexual, to pretend not to be, and to encourage the denunciation of those suspected to be.

Uncle Frédo had laughed at this. A man who hardly ever laughed. All that wasted energy, all that blindness, all those denials for absolutely nothing.

Cannibal 2.0 had been killed. All the members of his gang had been wishing for it. You had to be careful saying "all" around here; "all" meant the head honchos, the intimidating ones who broke innocent people's bones and burned anyone who didn't share their opinions.

Cannibal 2.0 was a nasty piece of work who had eaten a chunk of human flesh in front of the camera. He had left his criminal comrades speechless, and fabricated a legend that would crumble quickly. You rarely saw a gangster in love who couldn't get the object of his affection to stay at his side, especially when he was the Boss. He hadn't been able to convince Patience, and her departure had destroyed him to the point where he couldn't function like a proper criminal. Apart from hijacking freight trucks, which any small-time gangster could do, and which the police were powerless to stop, the Cité of Divine Power gang had achieved nothing. Cannibal had no political influence. In the last few months, not one important politician had come to ask for his support. Nothing.

Cannibal 2.0 had spent his time being squeezed for money by clever hustlers who pretended to know where Patience was. Three times he dragged his men to neighborhoods in Delmas, Cul-de-Sac Plain, and Croix-des-Bouquets. They'd entered whatever house the informer had pointed to, terrorized and beaten the people they found inside, who'd never even heard of a woman named Patience. People whispered in the Cité, and laughed behind Cannibal's back. Livio held his tongue during the vigils for fear of ending up like Fatal. Dodo the Drinker launched into loud laughter whenever he walked past the gang headquarters, and when Élise was good and tipsy she would repeat "love, love, love" over and over. It was more than his men could tolerate. Their policy, their way of life, their economy. It was all under threat.

Justin – that was Cannibal 2.0's Christian name – had been killed while he was on the toilet. He had been vigilant. No armed person could approach him. He knew how he would end up. Like Joël, like Freddy, and so many others before them. He protected himself, and imagined every scenario that could lead to his being taken out. He'd trusted no one. He was smart enough to divvy up the spoils with the rest of the gang, but they needed more than that. Even the police seemed to have forgotten them. They'd all listened to Dread Bob on the radio while their leader moped.

Rumor had it that Jules César had unloaded his gun through the toilet door. He was working with the dreadlocked guy who was one of the few able to approach Cannibal 2.0. When the others realized what was happening, they'd showed up laughing loudly, dripping sweat and cruelty and fed up as hell. They'd taken turns firing their weapons through the door of the shitter.

The photo of the violently dethroned king made the rounds. The bullet-riddled corpse, the mangled head. Photos of corpses were always repulsive. When it was a violent death, a murder, they forced people to reflect on the nature of human beings, on the role of the State and justice. And I'd seen my fair share of corpses in my life. My grandmother's body beside me in the bed, bodies devoured by dogs, young people whose corpses were in such good condition that I sincerely questioned if they were truly dead, beheaded and burned bodies, newborns tossed by their mothers into trash cans or the ravines because they couldn't take care of them, because they were afraid of the reaction of their parents, of members of their church, and on which the animals feasted, and the body of my friend Pierrot, but this man transformed into a sieve, his pants down, ass filled with shit, the shards of the toilet bowl blown to smithereens by bullets around him and in his body... I'd never seen that. The indignity that went with his take-down got to me.

The photo had been shared over WhatsApp and commented on thousands of times. I abstained. I needed to find something more original. The Cité of Divine Power's new strongman. The general himself. Jules César. I had his phone number. I dared. He picked up.

"Cécé, *sa k pase?*"

"I'm fine... What about you?

Jules César's voice was different. The voice of a Boss who wants you to know it. He agreed to let me come see him, apparently not holding it against me for ditching him the last time at Morel's. He'd let the guys know I was coming. A young man I'd never seen before, a little chubby, opened up right away to let me into the base. Jules César was slumped in the rocking chair where Patience had sat the time Joël had summoned me. He wore Ray-Bans with mirrored lenses. When you became Boss, stuff would miraculously just fall into your hands. He'd only been in charge since yesterday and he was already sporting the external markers that indicated his rank. I doubted that he had inherited all that from Cannibal 2.0.

A glass of Coca-Cola with ice was on the coffee table. It was the first time I'd seen Jules drink anything other than beer. All of a sudden I was thirsty. The boss clicked his fingers and one minute later, I had a Coke too, served by a young woman I'd never noticed before in the Cité.

"So, Cécé, what can I do for you?"

"Umm... I wanted to congratulate you personally, and also take a photo of you for social media. The public doesn't know the new Boss of the Cité of Divine Power yet."

He took off his sunglasses and sat up in the chair. No one, I assumed, would ever call him Cassave again. His shirt was three quarters of the way open and I could see his hairless chest. He made a sulky pout and finally said, "Why not?"

He put his sunglasses back on, and positioned himself in the chair while I snapped away at him with my phone.

"That's good, Cécé. You've taken enough."

I looked at the photos, pretty satisfied, and picked one that I posted on Instagram immediately. The reactions would flood in soon enough. I'd evaluate the damage later. I started drinking my cola, getting ready to listen to Jules César. As of yesterday, he must have begun yapping even more than usual. I didn't wait long.

"I'm going to change this cité, Cécé. No one here was happy with Cannibal. As you know, I never forgave him for murdering Pierrot. I wish my mom was here to see me. Guerda would be proud of her son, I can tell you that much! I'm going to look after the children and women. I'm going to force politicians to pay attention to us. Public funds need to be spent on the people. The senators and deputies will have to come and negotiate."

He paused for a moment, took off his glasses, his eyes shining, and added:

"Even the President of the Republic will have to come here if he wants to see out his mandate."

I almost choked. An ice cube had slipped inside my mouth by accident, but as Grand Ma used to say, things don't happen for no reason. I was spared having to respond. I noisily crunched the ice cube as I smiled. The dreadlocks guy, a natural traitor, raised his right thumb in a sign of approval. I could have asked Jules César how he was planning to go about things. I could have told him that Freddy, Joël, and Cannibal had all said pretty much the same things, that assuming his status as a gangster who would soon be killed by one of his own men might serve him better, that he should enjoy every second of his life whose days were numbered. But it was better that we stayed on good terms.

The new Boss had three cell phones that Dreadlocks managed. They wouldn't stop ringing, and each time he would answer saying that the Boss was busy, to call back later. In the end, he did interrupt him – it must have been someone important – and whispered into his ear before passing him the cell phone. Before he brought it to his ear, the Boss said to me, "Cécé, *n a wè yon lòt lè*. Cécé, we'll see each other another time."

It had been raining for three days. The alleys were flooded, the women in a bad mood. They did what they could to clean the porches, the bedrooms, the clothes and utensils that would never be clean because cleanliness is hard to achieve. No sooner done than undone. The argument that we were cursed was plausible. Everything had been tossed. Some thoughtless hand had hurled hundreds of shacks into space, just mess upon mess. We stumbled over plastic bottles that hadn't found their way to the nearby sea, already filled with garbage. It rained, and we were bogged down in our lives. There was mud on our feet, our clothes, our hands. Maybe our souls too.

Women hit their children, their husbands hit them, kids beat up on each other, and neighbors got into shouting matches for the slightest reason; cries resounded from every direction as over our heads massive clouds gathered, portending various catastrophes, mini ends of the world, ruptures.

Soline was possessed. She had lost control of her body. Swaying left to right, she chanted religious songs, a blissful little smile on her face.

Her swollen stomach indicated that she was sick with something. She looked pregnant, even. She no longer sold her garlic by the side of the road – she didn't have the energy to compete with younger women. She'd said nothing to me about it, but I suspected she'd been insulted, even pushed around by one of them.

Now she spent almost all of her time sitting on her little porch with her worn-out tray made from fan palm leaves that held a scattering of garlic bulbs that couldn't be sold because they were half rotten, beside a plastic tub containing the products I had given her. Thankfully, people actually bought those. After every sale she would bring me the money she made and say I could give her whatever I wanted. I'd tell her to keep it all, and give her more stuff to sell. She raised her arms to the sky and intoned a chant to the glory of her God, whom she asked to protect me. All conversations with Soline now drifted to God and religion. I couldn't even get her to talk about Grand'Anse, her sister, her idyllic childhood near a river amid trees and happy bands of children about whose fates she knew nothing. Everything had changed too much, and too much for the worse, so we left behind our memories and our voices on the road of misfortune.

Uncle Frédo never brought up his memories. He never spoke. He expressed himself only with grunts and tender little smiles. Alcohol drowned everything, burned everything. I asked him once to tell me about the United States, the country where he had lived for so long, and he sat down on the small bed, put his head in his hands, and said nothing until I left. Those moments of life were lost to him. That country had stripped him of himself. He didn't have the stuff of those who made it there by working twenty hours a day.

Lost corner of a lost country, a boil on the lip of a sick nation, the Cité of Divine Power had nonetheless let Frédo find peace. He was too skinny for a man his age, had to cinch the worn belt that kept his pants up around his stomach and ribs. His hair was thinning and his hairline receding. Tonton resembled a bird, in fact, though there were none left in the Cité. They'd been mercilessly hunted by starving teenagers who either ate them or tossed them down some alley when they weren't edible. He smiled when I told him he was too thin, as if to say that I was too.

Plus, everything was designed so that nothing and no one could escape. Pastor Victor, his wife Andrise, and many others told us to take care of our souls, not our bodies. And anyway, who would dream of dragging this cursed body to the kingdom of heaven? And only Heaven was worth the bother. Amen. An old refrain that sustained faith and let us forget. Ours was a restless sleep. So many obstacles between us and ourselves, obstacles of our own making.

What do I know about heartache? Other than it traps you in your body and your mind. Your obsession takes over, which gets the better of you in the end. When you think you're alive, you're only chasing shadows. You keep going, until you die one way or another. Death comes in many shapes.

Fany was buried alive by the memory of some crook she judged was better than an exuberant pastor who could have been of service to her soul, if she'd let him. Soline had made the wrong choice, and had nothing left but some outdated men's clothes to wrap around her body with her memories. Cannibal 2.0 destroyed his legend as a ruthless boss by chasing Patience like a lunatic, and murdering Pierrot for having let his captive go. I didn't know how much Carlos cared about me. Everything he said embarrassed me more than anything else. I no longer responded to his messages, his invitations to come live in Tabarre, the links he sent me on WhatsApp to songs that spoke of love, suffering, broken hearts, and reconciliation.

It was still raining and the general misery was poignant, endless sobs isolating the people of the Cité even further by swelling the disgusting gullies, forcing everyone to stay inside their hovels.

I was lying in bed, thinking about the thousands of "friends" I had in my phone, people I didn't know, who, depending on the day, insulted me or praised me. Their existence hinged on whether my phone's battery was charged or not, and on what I posted. I preferred the sound of raindrops falling from a hole in the sheet metal and into the aluminum pot I had put below it to gather the water and spare me from having to dry the gray cement floor. The steady tac-tac of rain dripping into the bowl soothed me like a lullaby. I fell asleep.

Jules César had instituted some new rules in the Cité. Large gatherings were forbidden. Even if there was a corpse in one of the alleys. In which case, there was now a number to call. Men would come for the body and leave quickly. The new boss also settled domestic disputes and conflicts between neighbors. In the former situation, if the girlfriend or wife was his type, he'd arrange private sessions with her. Peace in the home was important for balance in the Cité, he said, hidden behind the sunglasses that he never took off, even at night. He had banned the police from entering the Cité, except the ones who lived here, but they could only wear their uniforms outside the Cité.

  Anyone who ran any kind of business whatsoever had to make a weekly payment to compensate for the protection he granted them. Gang members now had flashy new motorbikes they rode through the alleys, arbitrarily taxing people with little shops or stands. I gave what I could. For me and Tonton. They came by often, sometimes twice a week. I was considered a friend of Jules, which I'm sure helped. The Boss made a point of coming over to say hello when he was out patrolling with his men. He'd bang on the wooden door, shouting my name. I'd come out to see him on the porch. I didn't want him coming in, didn't want any confusion about our relationship. His reputation as a ladies' man was established, even if with my little girl body I wasn't worth much sexually speaking. I didn't know how to say hello to him or what to say. After "*Sa k pase, sa k ap fèt?*" I'd go quiet. I felt other people's eyes on us. But no one was allowed to watch or say a word. Jules's long, slim body took up the whole porch, his head almost touching the roof; I felt crushed by his presence and wondered how I would remember him when he was dead. He kept his gun conspicuous in a holster on his right hip, and he was well-groomed, unlike lots of his men, like the one charged with carrying his cell phones which rang every fifteen seconds. He knew he was supposed to interrupt the boss only with very important people, meaning the ones who helped maintain the slums in a state of terror.

Jules wanted to know if I still went to Morel's – which could have been a viable conversation topic. I didn't go there anymore. Jules told me he was very busy, that running the Cité of Divine Power was a lot of work, especially since his predecessors had done nothing. He was surprised by the number of conflicts he had to mediate, and the sanctions he had to impose, on men in particular. He alone embodied multiple government institutions.

I had heard this same speech from his predecessors. He put his hand on my shoulder like an old friend. I smiled. I called him Jules, and he smiled too. It must have been a long time since he'd heard himself referred to as anything other than "*Chèf la*," It must have been tough for a criminal who didn't want people to forget that he had a mother he loved, even in the hereafter.

I remembered the night Jules César had cried. Maybe that was the invisible connection he felt with me. After all, he couldn't talk about his mother or his journey to the guys walking behind him and wishing every second that they could kill him and take his place, much less the rich politicians who met with him in secret. It would have been considered inappropriate, or distasteful, having nothing to do with the daily violence required to instill fear and stay alive. Jules César didn't know what friendship was. He was at the end of his story. Behind all the veils, all the pretending, death was all there was. He knew that. Which was also why his position, beyond its downsides, brought extreme pleasure. The privilege of having money. Of being the person who can squeeze money out of others, as "tax." The person who relieves truck drivers of their merchandise. The person who blackmails officials who represent a government feeble to the point of caricature. The person who decides whether vendors and entrepreneurs are authorized to circulate and work. The privilege to profit, abuse, and humiliate. The women whom Jules saw to arbitrate matters of peace and justice would leave utterly defeated, sinking into a deep dark hole they would never leave, weakened in the great daily struggle they waged to live and keep their children alive. Of course the Boss was insatiable: he satisfied not only his own appetites but those of his family and friends who had died of various deprivations.

Victor was desperately trying to get me to go to church. He knocked on my door one Friday morning, Bible under his left arm. I offered him Grand Ma's rocking chair and sat next to him on the iron chair that squeaked. As he spoke, he was looking at the house facing mine, which concealed Fany's body and eyes from him.

Victor was a concentrate of those lives, those bodies, those souls born into defeat, and who silently resigned themselves. He looked exhausted. But he didn't complain. He was carrying out his mission in life, was widely respected, an apostle of God, and he brought in white missionaries from every corner of the United States, well-meaning folks in white T-shirts on which was written "Jesus loves Haiti" or "Haiti is for Jesus," who cried at our poverty but understood the utility of our misery when it came to selling the promise of an eternal and better life in the Kingdom of Christ. Victor was born here, but he had understood that religion was a good springboard to getting out.

He was plagued by doubt, and in physical pain, wringing his hands to the point of injury, his body crying out for Fany.

He had been married for sixteen years to Andrise, a good Christian who had brought five children into the world – Jonas, Sarah, David, Esther, and Ruth – born obedient and full of God's promise. And that was his happiness, until he saw Fany, before she reminded him of his humanity. Fany had unknowingly shaken up his entire being. Now the good pastor couldn't tell if his desperate desire to talk to her meant he was losing or saving his soul.

Victor was a sober man, in every respect. He didn't want to frighten Fany or impose himself on her. Maybe he was grateful to her for unsettling him and showing him that man is always one step behind his desires, unable to vanquish his nature. Andrise had understood but surely had never mentioned it. After all, her husband hadn't done anything. He had just been robbed of some of his convictions, and it weakened him. Fany no longer came to church, and Andrise had become sad, her scarves lost much of their gaiety.

Victor asked me if I would use my social media accounts to draw more young people to the church. His son Jonas had told him I was the only one around here whose posts attracted so much interest. I told him I'd think about it. He liked my answer. He would come back to sit on the porch facing the house on whose stoop Fany would appear one day, while he was there. In the meantime, there were the plants and there was Élise. Nothing got past her. Not love, not sadness, not despair.

Yvrose had closed her shop. She wore her widowhood like a badge. The color black and her thinness combined to give her a tragic air. Her hair had completely and miraculously turned white. She was an old lady now. She kept the shop going until there was nothing left on the shelves, apart from the grime of years gone by. Life-dust, old stains that told of days full of laughter and worry, the presence of a husband, of two sons who lived on the other half of the island, a neighbor country yet so different. I'd heard lots of stories, growing up, of racism and massacres in the Dominican Republic.

Would those boys ever come back? They didn't know themselves. The travelers had no say over their own lives, so their desires were meaningless. Uncle Frédo had come back from his American interlude with his head and his gaze full of silence, and his liver full of alcohol. Yvrose went to church and asked everyone to pray that Fénelon's soul rest in peace. Did he even have a soul? She might have known that certain women cursed him, that his legacy was the great despair they felt, the kind you don't speak about or recover from. Yes, souls must need rest after a life that's tormented their bodies, which were simply trying to do what they were meant to – live – while the mind is ravaged by wanting and the need to be something other than yourself. Which is surely why people prayed so much. I was slightly embarrassed to still feel such disgust when I thought about Fénelon. There were lots of people like him in the Cité. The poverty drove everyone mad – women, men, and animals alike.

Sister Julienne, pulled along by nostalgia, or emptiness, slowly vanished, buried by the passing time. She'd been seen only rarely since Freddy disappeared, gradually consumed by a mixture of shame and maternal love. It changed her. She would hide her face with a straw hat and her thin body swam in her ample dresses. No one can outrun their regrets. Her doubts, her hurts, her hustle and bustle deceived no one, not even herself.

The silence imposed by death often isn't a real one. It doesn't settle. Freddy was in the past. Even the red graffiti goodbye messages sprayed on walls faded or were covered by other tags. And meanwhile, several bosses had gone the same route, had occupied that rickety, arbitrary, and much-coveted throne.

Amid the chaos of lives and messages, one stumble after another, Yvrose was part of a story that left no imprint, an image streaming by that no one noticed or remembered. She was a woman swept along by life who followed the current without understanding, and without asking for anything either.

Nestor's old hand had lost none of its precision. The heart beats in time with the hammer's steady tap-tap. A thousand, two thousand, maybe more, of those chiseled and tenderly varnished wooden boxes freeze moments of regret, of constantly questioning the past, the present, and the future. Now that not much of the future remained, nothing was left of the past. Nestor would surely die without seeing Louisa again, who still didn't have her papers, a prisoner, happily perhaps, of extravagant America. He had been able to see her on Fatal's phone, and he'd been moved to tears. She was so much like her mother, the same boisterous, joyous laugh that brought tears to his eyes. She had put on weight. Must be plenty of food where she was. He had mixed feelings about his two granddaughters, who were seven and four. He couldn't talk to them because all they could say in Creole was *kòman ou ye, papi?* (how are you, grandpa?) He'd wave his right hand at that, smiling discreetly so they wouldn't see that he was missing his front teeth. Louisa was full of enthusiasm, always promising to send more money to her old father, but only sending a hundred dollars, three times a year. It was tough for her. Alongside the afternoon courses she was taking to become a nurse, she worked mornings in a nursing home where she wiped old folks' butts, and slept four nights a week away from home to care for a rich old woman. She was paid minimum wage, slept in a chair monitoring the woman's breathing and giving her medication at precise hours. Her husband – she had told Nestor they were married, but he'd never seen photos of the ceremony and didn't ask too many questions so as not to upset Louisa – worked on construction sites during the day, and took care of the little girls the rest of the time. Nestor didn't like him. Though what difference could it make? The husband called him "Father Nestor," which bothered him a lot.

He sensed that he would die without ever seeing his daughter again. Little Daniel had gone too soon. He'd known his son was lost the day he learned he was a member of Fat Élie's gang. Gangsters didn't live very long. They reached the peak of gratification with their weapons, the money they stole, the way in which they disposed of people's lives, but it was always brief. Daniel had always been a good boy, too attached to his mother. It was her death, actually, that upset him so much that he embraced the criminal life. Fat Élie had had the corpse brought to Nestor in the Cité of Divine Power. He hadn't even finished mourning his wife and there he was burying his son, on the quiet. Daniel had been killed by the police. Nestor had refused the gang leader's money for the burial, had also refused to let anyone come to his house. He was happy to make a decision on the kid's behalf, for the first time in years. Since then, he woke up in the middle of every night, wondering where he'd gone wrong and why it wasn't his son in Fatal's place, making those cheap trinkets that had somehow allowed his father to feed him and his sister.

Fatal was a blessing to him. He'd come from Saint-Jean du Sud, his hometown. He was the son of a distant cousin. Nestor had suggested that he come to Port-au-Prince when he met him at the cousin's funeral, at the church of Saint-Jean. He was a country boy, easygoing, hard-working, always ready to pitch in. Nestor had been terrified when Cannibal 2.0 had him beaten up. He treated his injuries and explained to Fatal that people who kept their mouths shut around here got to live as long as him. The boy had understood.

Old Nestor and Fatal together formed quite the orchestra. They'd bang their hammers from morning 'til night in beautiful harmony behind the house. And to think their suffering went unheard, even when it rose in volume, just slightly louder than the racket that kept them alive.

His name was Philippe, but we had always called him Pipo. He was gentle, he liked plants, and Fany had fallen in love with him at first sight. He could have popped out of one of the romance novels she used to read as a teenager. He'd been with lots of women before her. He had fathered four children, with four different women, whom he rarely saw. His exes made his life miserable, he told Fany. And she believed him. She believed everything he told her. Pipo swore to her that all the women who called her up to badmouth him and urge her to drop him before it was too late were crazy. He was her man, and nothing would ever change that.

Two rival gangs shared Bethlehem. Not a day went by without someone dying. Pipo would talk about fallen friends, staring into nothing, almost as if he felt his own death approaching. He was close with Fanfan le Sauvage, they were cousins. Pipo wasn't meant for the front lines. He should never have died.

That night, he didn't come home. Surely because of the fighting. The gunfire got heavier, it was the final battle. There could only be one boss in Bethlehem.

Fanfan won. Franzy Petit Poignet ended up lynched. Around thirty people were killed, soldiers from both sides, and others to top it off, as usual. Pipo was dead but that didn't prevent Fanfan from celebrating his victory and the beginning of his undisputed reign over Bethlehem. Pipo became a rumor. No one came to Fany to tell her that the love of her life had died. No one thought it worth their while to console her. Fanfan made payments to the mothers of Pipo's children, but nobody acknowledged Fany's grief. There was no sound to her grief. Even in front of her sister, Élise, who didn't even bother to listen when Fany told her that she and Pipo had planned to get married. Fany left Bethlehem, consumed by grief, in part to escape the mockery of those who knew all about Pipo's many fiancées. Élise followed her sister. She was nothing without Fany, never had been. Élise was the troubled one, the alcoholic, but she was also the one who shook her sister awake in the middle of the night when she orgasmed too intensely before Pipo's imagined intimate assaults.

Fany was the pretty one, too beautiful for Pipo, thought Élise. But everything Élise thought was dead on arrival, it vanished before she could even express it. She had always been like that. She was content to drink and smoke her life away, hiding behind the same plants that failed to cure her sister. Because, ultimately, the only disease the sisters suffered from was each other, and themselves.

Livio and Soline were my memories. They were close to Grand Ma. I didn't know anything about Livio. He was poor, like most everyone in the Cité, knew a thing or two about water, about death, and about joy too. He danced to the blare of projectiles, knowing it would invariably give him the opportunity to talk about the Cité and the country as he saw them. He could talk shit about anyone – apart from the Cité's top dog of the moment – the president, the chief of police, the politicians. He spoke of a country jeopardized by dwindlings and disappearances, and of an Africa from which he'd inherited a few scraps, remnants of songs from a crossing too long and exhausting to recover from.

Maybe Livio never had dreams, a dream of leaving like Tonton, a dream of a better life, of serenity, like Carlos, but he had hope. He told a truth that I picked up in the middle of his sometimes-muddled stories.

Everything can dissolve. Friendship. Love. We're children of oblivion. I hadn't heard from Carlos again. That was what I wanted. He'd been at his wits' end trying to convince me to follow him. He wasn't part of the freedom inside me, he had tried too hard to put himself between me and the outside world. No one could prevent me from watching, from touching even, the violence that stared us in the face every morning. Some days, I would start looking for traces of Grand Ma in the house and in the alleyways, things she would have looked at, voices that would have made her smile, but everything was changing and there was nothing I could do to influence that. Félicienne's stall was gone. She now lived with her son in the States – for health reasons, supposedly. Her daughter-in-law sold, in the same spot, secondhand clothes that she had hung on nails and hangers over the entire front wall of the house. It made my heart ache, for a moment, but life here was quicksand, you had to grasp the transience of things and get used to it. Maybe nobody, apart from Soline, who was losing her mind a little, and Uncle Frédo and me remembered my grandmother. Whenever I ran into Maître Jean-Claude, blinking his eyes behind large glasses, he would ask me, in French, to say hello to my grandmother. I'd quickly tell him I would. Either he'd forgotten or had never heard that she'd died. He froze people in their first reality, and left them there, one of many who saw nothing and heard nothing.

Days went by, then the nights, death resumed. Intractable. Decomposing bodies in the ravine beds or on vacant land, blending into the garbage, both witnesses to a period of time ripped to shreds so no memory of it would survive. None at all. Dodo, in his alcohol-induced delirium, used to say that life was here and now. There'd been so many bosses, seconds-in-commands, lackeys, politicians, and business people who made their way down the rot-filled alleys toward gang headquarters. All those bills meant to corrupt had poisoned everyone, especially the poor, like him and Lorette. The ones who stopped needing anything in the end, taking refuge in alcohol and lunacy, solitary spaces, observation posts.

Jules César will die soon. He said so himself yesterday, on a radio broadcast that made the rounds on social media, arousing admiration and indignation. The police had put a price on his head. Everyone knew where to find him, but no one could come get him.

    I kept posting photos. I needed as many people as possible to "like" my page and comment on its contents. I was in the race to exist more than ever before. I imposed what I saw and heard on others. I also received voice memos, images, and videos, often from people I didn't know. Exist only for yourself in spite of and to the detriment of anyone else. I considered anyone who solicited my friendship, followed me, "liked" me or simply bothered to read or comment on my posts – even negatively – as part of my loot. They helped keep my accounts active, trending. Catherine Paris continued to pay me and supply me with products, and Jules César kept calling to ask me what I thought, what others thought, with a hint of worry in his voice. He considered me well-respected, thought I could be a popular First Lady, and asked me to join the group.

Natacha hadn't come back after she gave birth. She had taken over her mother's business, selling skin-whitening products. The soldier's life had left her with nothing but memories of sexual harassment, the sun on her fragile skin, a 12-gauge, sawed-off shotgun that was too heavy. Cumbersome. Just like the stroke of bad luck of being born in the Cité of Divine Power and this endless chaotic journey she was on with no end in sight, and the children she'd never really wanted and to whom she couldn't explain why this was the way it was. It all made her scream with such rage that she beat them as hard as she could, the way her mother had beaten her. Natacha would have liked to be young. Nothing more. No longer to have to lock eyes with the lonely and tired woman she'd become in that seven by nine-inch mirror, framed in blue plastic and cracked down the middle, into which she looked several times a day.

She had believed her life could change, she'd told me the last time I ran into her on the main street, her newborn in her arms. A little respect, some money for herself and her children. Very quickly, she'd been assigned only thankless tasks. Feeding kidnapped persons whose ransoms hadn't been paid yet, confronted with their sufferings and their begging. It was this baby, unwanted like the others, that had allowed her to escape. He was wrapped in a yellow towel, sleeping peacefully, as if he knew he needed to stockpile rest for the tumult to come. I hadn't dared ask Natacha who the father was. The question didn't matter much in the Cité, where the good Lord was daddy to all the children, watching over their well-being. Conception was merely a detail.

Jules César had said on the radio that the people needed to be saved, and that he knew how to go about it. Then he explained his death as the event that would change everything. No one gets named Jules César by chance, he said, before listing every step that had gotten him to the top. He'd gone to college, had even had a loving mother who had been taken from him by poverty, disorganization, and marginalization.

Feeling death approaching, Jules César was merciless with the residents of the Cité. They had to pay more and more for the so-called protection he offered them. Without him, they were nothing, he would say, the authorities would roll right in here and do whatever they wanted. Thanks to him, the Cité was talked about on the news, even abroad, and there was a price to pay for that.

Jules's voice was part of the noise. The kind that doesn't even have an echo. I was being sent clips on WhatsApp multiple times a day of his flashy proclamations. Behind his sunglasses you could see him, lit up, but deep down very sad. Or rather, there was a nostalgia about him, the kind desperate people have. That's actually how you can recognize them, the ones who break, kill, and burn because the future is hazy.

Uncle Frédo was a shadow, and I was the shadow of his shadow. I had taken a picture of the two of us that I set as the home screen on my cell phone. The photo was nice, but we looked lifeless. Behind our bony faces hid a thousand upheavals, a thousand untellable stories. Like Natacha, I didn't look young either. What I called youth was a form of joy, the satisfaction of being alive, the feeling that the viable part of the world passed through our bodies. A fire. We were living in a suspicious calm that not even the projectiles or the bad news could penetrate anymore.

Tonton had returned from his obstacle course. Out of breath. Little by little I was grasping that he too had rejected America, that much-desired foreign land that had wanted nothing to do with him, that hadn't made room for him because he didn't have his papers. He would never get his documents and he thought that was just fine. The maps are drawn so that certain people who get lost never find their way in this vast world. The photo came to life when I looked at it, it had captured everything. The setting sun, the scrubbed-down walls of the houses. I posted it on social media. Ten, twenty, a hundred and twenty people liked it. It's true that we like things, or even love them, for no reason. For nothing at all.

archipelago books
is a non-profit publisher devoted to
promoting cross-cultural exchange through innovative
classic and contemporary international literature
archipelagobooks.org

elsewhere editions
translates luminous picture books from around the world
elsewhereeditions.org